REVIVING SUNSHINE

A Novel by
Sarah Eads

For information, or to order additional copies, please contact:

Beacon Publishing Group
P.O. Box 41573 Charleston, S.C., 29423
800.817.8480 / beaconpublishinggroup.com

Publisher's catalog available upon request.

ISBN-13: 978-1-949472-70-7

ISBN-10: 1-949472-70-1

Published in 2019. New York, NY 10001.

First Edition. Printed in the USA.

Reviving Sunshine is dedicated to the two Italian musicians, Eros Ramazzotti and Biagio Antonacci, whose music inspired me to write a story that hopefully will provide sunshine during struggles of life.

CHAPTER ONE

He looked at his watch constantly and waited for the train, as he was heading to a meeting to discuss his future in an industry where hipsters and wannabes were plaguing like locusts. He spent thirty years clawing his way through the good, bad and the ugly, and now all the new kids sang on TV and got a deal. It was sickening, and he was being pushed around like an old, incompetent senior in a nursing home.

Years were showing on his face on the occasional days, but lack of sleep did that to a man of his age. He stuffed his hands into his tight, dark-washed jeans pocket. He was a casual and laid-back man, who lived in the city where he felt respected for what he did for a living; it made him feel at home.

The city-transit pulled up to the small outskirt town depot, and he lifted his worn-out messenger bag. His hazel colored eyes stared at the train, as it screeched to a halt and hissed at its future passengers to stand away from the opening doors. He watched as several regulars smiled at him and greeted him by first name instead of calling him by his last. He had become friends with many of the old-timers that often challenged him to chess at the park.

"Ciao, Chudamani!" An older man walked off.

Chudamani walked over and gave him a hand while others walked around him. He looked at the older man, who smiled at Chudamani with an almost toothless smile.

"You must meet my daughter; she's a pretty girl now." The older man patted his cheek.

"She is married, remember, Giorgio? She married the shop keeper's son up from the main road." Chudamani chuckled a little.

"Well, then, I guess you are too late. But you really should marry and get some meat on those skinny legs." Giorgio tapped his leg.

"Eventually. I am much too busy to settle." Chudamani patted the old man's shoulder.

The warning whistle sounded, and Chudamani wished the older man a good day before leaping onto the train. He held onto the flimsy strap above an older woman, who smiled.

"Why aren't you married, Chudamani?" She asked, as she held onto her purse. "You are getting too old to play music."

"Why haven't you asked me?" He teased her.

She gave him a look and laughed. "You aren't my type, Chudamani. I like them extremely young, like my neighbor's son across the hall from me. He's twenty-three and looks like a Roman god that has become mortal."

"I'll win you over, signora, watch." He chuckled.

The old, white-haired woman tried to keep her wits about her, as she flirted everyday with him. He listened about the fantasy that she and her neighbor's son played out with denying feelings for the older woman. It was amusing to hear; then, there was always someone who reminded him of the past.

"Hey, Chudamani, isn't that the girl you were supposed to marry just six months ago?" A middle-aged man pointed to the paper.

Chudamani glanced over at the picture of the Italian model. She'd married another Italian singer who traveled in the same circle as she did; the younger man was more fitting for the her than he was. Chudamani took a deep breath and shrugged.

"No matter," he answered.

"She's got her a younger twit," the gruff-looking passenger hacked.

"As long as she's happy." Chudamani glanced at the watch on his right wrist. "I got time."

"Not much." The middle-aged man laughed.

"Maybe a little more than you if you keep smoking those death sticks."

The car laughed at his witty come back, and the middle age man wrinkled his rounded nose on his large head. Chudamani was always a smart-ass to certain people on his commute to the city. It kept him fresh and full of new material.

The city-transit train pulled into the Roman station, and Chudamani stepped out first. He stepped to the side and helped the older lady that he stood in front of.

"You need to marry a beautiful Italian woman who can respect that strong back and good heart, Chudamani. I'll keep an eye open for her and send her your way." The older lady smiled and patted his cheek. "Maybe you need to eat more; you are too skinny."

"Grazia, signora," he said, before leading with his best foot.

He slipped the hundred fifty Euro sunglasses on and kept a fast pace to make it into the meeting on time. His long legs carried him to the underground train, which he took to the next stop by the Roman Forum. Crowded with foreigners at the time, he was slowed down and had to leap over the railing to get ahead of the camera-carriers and walkers. He was nimble for his tender age of fifty-something.

"Buongiorno, Chudamani," the young women at the corner flower shop cat-called.

He simply blew a kiss, and they fought for the invisible kiss. He grabbed a paper and stared at the entertainment section with the great announcement that the youth of the industry were turning out new music, making older singers obsolete.

"It isn't true, Chudamani. You still got the skill," the newsstand owner said.

"Grazie, signore," he said, as he paid him for the paper.

The next headline read: *Chudamani Amoretto Sitting on Thin Ice.*

He walked briskly as he read the paper, not paying attention to where he was walking. He stepped off the curb and heard a nervous honking sound. He glanced up to see the taxi cab coming at him.

As he stepped back onto the curb, he bumped into someone. He turned and looked at the young woman, who was wide-mouthed and covered in coffee. He stepped back as she cursed in her native language, unfamiliar to him.

"Now, I'm going to be late because someone couldn't watch where they were going," she muttered, picking up the cups. "And I'm going to get cited for littering a beautiful street. How am I going afford to buy Italian coffee?"

He knelt and picked up cups and napkins from the fine gourmet café around the corner. He looked at the distraught young woman, who seemed to be displeased in what happened. He reached for some napkins.

"Scusa," he said.

She looked up and adjusted her dark frame, designer sunglasses on her face. She stared at him with a deep frown of displeasure.

"Oh, you only offer me a napkin. My boss is going to kill me because his coffee is late. Chauvinistic pigs that work at the corner office. I hardly fit in already, so, great, let's spill coffee on the American!" She snatched the napkin and dabbed her face.

"Cosa, non capisco," Chudamani remarked, as he started dabbing the coffee off her shirt.

"Hey, watch your hands, garcon," she snapped and slapped his hand away from her bust. "The merchandise isn't for sale."

"Danielle, we're going to be late!" Another woman's voice came up. "What happened?"

"Someone decided to not look where they leapt." Danielle looked at him.

"Geez." The dark-haired woman rolled her eyes.

The next thing that happened were two Italians shouting at each other about what happened. Chudamani snapped at her, and the younger woman slapped him across the face. He cursed her out and pointed to Danielle.

"Hey, I'm not clumsy," Danielle stated. "You ran into me because you had blinders on."

"Che?" He questioned.

Danielle stood up and nodded. "Yes, I can understand your language. You people don't look when you are in a hurry."

He looked at her Italian friend, as she folded her arms and nodded. He blew them off after he gave his quick apology to Danielle.

"Don't mind him; he's just got a stick up his ass because his fiancée left him for someone younger!" Her friend shouted.

He glanced over and flipped her off, Italian style.

"I have a change of clothes that may fit you, or a jacket. Whichever you feel comfortable in, Danielle."

"Thanks, Fiorella, but I'll be fine. I just need to go get more coffee," Danielle said, as she wiped her sunglasses. "I figured I'd bump into some Italian hot shot sometime."

Fiorella smiled and tossed the rest of the coffee in a nearby trash can. The two women walked into the old building, and the receptionist looked at them.

"Coffee accident, again, Danielle?" the polished woman asked.

"Go jump off a cliff, Pietra," Fiorella spat.

"Defending your little American pet, Fiorella? She'll never learn to be like us in this business. And, the way she dresses, she'll never be married." The overly-gorgeous woman painted her lips.

Fiorella rolled her eyes, while Danielle stared at Pietra.

"She's always made up, even for stupid meetings," Danielle whispered.

"She's a cardboard cutout of what a chauvinist world wants. If you have your boobs done and suck the big one, you get ahead." Fiorella narrowed her eyes at Pietra. "She's slept with every client this label has except Chudamani Amoretto. He's pretty picky, even when it comes to girls like her." Fiorella slid her card, and the elevator door opened.

Danielle sighed and looked at Fiorella, as the five foot nine beauty—not an ounce of fat—talked about a girl just like herself.

"Do you know what this meeting is about?" Danielle asked.

"You're getting a client," Fiorella said. "About to use those translation skills. There's some American money makers investing in a client and buying out *his* contract. He's going to need a talking piece."

"Who is my client?"

Chudamani looked at his manager, as he talked to other clients. He stood up and stared out the window.

"I don't need a translator," Chudamani said. "I need a deal."

"And you are going to get a deal, Chudamani. We just need to play the part. You deal with this translator for a year and let him show you around the states a little. Come back and say Italy has the best in the world, and we all go home."

"Why am I being punished? I hate being sold to the highest bidder. I'm not anyone's property. I've been with you and this label for thirty years. Why change?"

"Change is good, Chudamani. It's better than dumping you in the streets, making you use your own money to advance your career in a new world where kids get information before you can wipe your ass in the morning."

"Crude, but point taken."

"Take the damn hat off and grow some hair," his manager, Antonio, ripped off the knit sock hat. "You look like a wannabe twit."

The glass doors opened, and three large men dressed in three-piece suits waddled in. Chudamani looked at Antonio and shook his head. He glanced over at the balding men that obviously didn't miss meals or have wives.

"Waiting on our translator," they said loudly and slowly.

The glass doors opened, and all looked over at Fiorella and Danielle. Chudamani looked at her, and she narrowed her eyes at him.

"I'm sorry, I must have the wrong room," Danielle said, walking to the doors.

Fiorella grabbed her and shook her head.

"Why is he here?" Danielle questioned through gritted teeth.

Fiorella smiled and stood straight. "He's your client, Danielle."

"Great!" Danielle faked her excitement.

She fixed the blazer that barely cover the coffee stains. She took a deep breath and stood up straight to walk to the glass table. She did not look at Chudamani directly, but she watched his reflection on the table.

"Ms. Bennet, I'm grateful that you were available to be here and meet signor Chudamani Amoretto; he's extended his career to the states. He also needs someone who can help him transition through the language barrier." The older man looked at Chudamani.

"Of course," Danielle said simply. "I believe he's familiar with 'vai a farti fottere!'

Chudamani narrowed his eyes at the American woman, who told him to 'go fuck himself'. He turned to Antonio and pointed to the woman. Antonio smirked, seeing that she'd be perfect for him.

"Perfetta, signora!" Antonio proudly expressed.

Danielle smiled and gave a nod of acknowledgment to the him. Chudamani slapped Antonio on the head. She looked at the three large men and smiled.

"See? I think our language barriers will be cleared up soon." Danielle folded her arms.

"Great! So, one year it is!"

"What!" Danielle questioned. "I just told him to go fuck himself, and you want me to spend a year with him?"

"Yes, that's exactly what we want you to do. Thank you for agreeing! If you fail to get him accustomed to the American culture, then you can pack your bags and move back to the swamps."

She looked at him, and he raised his brow at her.

"I'd be happy to help her out!" Fiorella stepped in.

"Who are you?"

"I'm Fiorella Mancini; I'm her assistant." Fiorella looked at Danielle and winked.

"Very well. There will be plenty of paperwork that will need to follow these two." The older man smiled. "Welcome aboard, and may this year be good to you."

"Bravo!" Antonio cheered. "Chudamani, andare."

He gave a groan and grabbed his messenger bag. He walked towards the glass doors and looked at Danielle as he walked past her. She folded her arms and pouted.

Antonio looked at them both and handed his card to Fiorella.

"In case you need help with grumpy over there," Antonio said.

"Oh, I think this is going to be fun," Fiorella said. "He's in good hands."

She clapped her hands, and he walked off. Danielle looked at the three older men.

"No one else wanted to work with him. He's the only singer in Italy that refuses to extend his tours to the States. It was obvious that he had issues with our language, but, thanks to you, he'll be ready to move on."

"Can't wait, sir!" Danielle's excitement was full of sarcasm.

"Ms. Bennet, I would change that shirt; it smells like coffee." The older man gave her a pat on the back. "Have a good day."

Danielle did a palm plant on her forehead, before she walked out. She looked at Fiorella, as her one, true Italian friend remained with a smile on her face.

"You are working with Chudamani Amoretto!" She nearly squealed with excitement. "Do you know what this means?"

"I may kill him before we start?"

"No, you just got a promotion!"

Danielle shook her head and walked down to her small office. Fiorella followed behind her and shut the door.

"So, what exactly are we supposed to do to get him ready?" Fiorella asked.

"I have research to do." Danielle looked at her. "You do realize he is just a guy, right? He's no god."

"Oh, Danielle, you are still unaware on how great this opportunity is. But do not worry, I am about to help you on this crazy journey to tame the dashing, talented Chudamani Amoretto!"

"Don't faint, Fiorella."

"We need to celebrate, and I know the best place." Fiorella smiled.

"No, I have to study my client's profile."

"Drinks at least," Fiorella said.

"Fine."

Chudamani walked along the Roman streets with less pep to his step, kicking loose pebbles on the sidewalk and whistling a little. He refused to work with a translator who was as stuck up as the one who was assigned to him.

He found himself walking to the last place he needed, but it was time to visit family. He walked into the century old Roman church and sat in the back pew. He knew the priest would find the lonely soul. His hazel eyes stared at the statues, which remained as mysterious as his future yet revealed so much more.

"It seems a stray dog has found his way home," a delighted voice said from the confessionals.

Chudamani looked at the young priest and removed his knit sock hat.

"You remembered—I don't have to smack the rest of your hair off," The young priest mentioned. "Chudamani, what's brought you to the house of God?"

"No confession for sure," Chudamani remarked. "I need advice."

"Mark this day that my big brother needs my guidance!" The younger man raised his hands upward.

Chudamani shook his head, and his little brother chuckled. He extended his hand to him, and Chudamani shook it.

"What can I do, brother?" He asked.

"I'm losing the belief that I am relevant in my industry. These American big shots from the label came and said I need to extend my reach to the States. And not only that, but they assigned a translator who will spend one year with me to 'teach' me the American ways. She's a cocky little girl, who must be color blind and has no fashion sense at all."

His brother looked at him and shook his head. There was a selfishness that his brother still fought with. He was pushing people out of his life because he believed he was God's gift to humanity.

"Well, maybe you need a break from dating only models. This American woman that is supposed to help you with her American ways, I say do something that scares you. Maybe you two can help each other. She sounds like she may need some advice from my good-looking brother, and you could see what she has to say." His brother smirked at him.

Chudamani looked at him and raised a brow.

"You haven't seen this woman. I mean, most American women care about what they look like, but this one looks like she rolled out of bed and threw a multi-colored quilt over her and called it 'fashion.' I'm convinced this woman wears a blanket to work," Chudamani mentioned. "She needs a miracle I don't think God can make."

"Chudamani," his brother gritted through his teeth.

"Sorry, brother, but…"

"Blinded by what true beauty is."

"Blinded with whatever she's wearing."

His brother looked at him and raised his dark brow. He shook his head and turned to him, his shallow brother, and smiled.

"I will pray that God takes the blinders off and guides you to the right path. Perhaps, you need to visit me more often."

"God has nothing to do with what I have to endure for the next year." Chudamani looked at his brother.

"Then go with God and find what he has planned for you this year. I will keep you in my thoughts and prayers. Maybe you need a little encouragement."

Chudamani put his hand out, and his brother shook his head. He wrapped his arms around his little brother before getting up.

"See you on Sunday, then?" his brother asked.

"Not ready to attend mass, padre," Chudamani remarked.

He gave a back-hand wave and walked out into the brisk Italian air. He slipped the knit sock hat on, before walking out into the busy Roman streets. He took a deep breath and walked with his usual strides. There was no one who was going to tell him how to live his life, and there was no way he was accepting the responsibilities of his actions…or that's what he thought.

CHAPTER TWO

The hard knock on his apartment door woke him from a deep sleep. His six-year-old Chocolate Labrador began to bark and rushed the front door. He rolled out of bed and slipped on a pair of dark washed jeans and the nearest shirt, before making it to the door.

"Portia, taci! Taci!" He hushed the dog.

He reached for the top lock and peeked through the peephole of the door. He rolled his eyes and opened the door to see Danielle standing there. He glanced at the patchwork skirt and long sleeve t-shirt. Her suede boots looked like she did arts and crafts with a blind man.

"Buongiorno, Scrooge," she said, holding up a bag with Italian pastries inside and coffee.

He stepped to the side, and she walked in and sat the morning delights on the kitchen counter. He watched as Portia wagged her tail and nuzzled the strange woman.

"Buongiorno," she greeted the lab.

She glanced up at him, as he felt betrayed by the only girl that was loyal to him. He whistled, and Portia sat down in front of Danielle. He whistled again, and Portia laid down.

"Traditore," Chudamani muttered.

Danielle smiled and stood up to look at the hazel-eyed, six foot three Italian. He towered over her five foot four figure and probably could throw her across the room if he wanted. He, of course, brushed past her and grabbed plates. His interest in learning English was far from his mind. He knew enough to ask the basic questions.

"Sit," he stated.

"So, you do speak English?" Danielle was surprised.

"Little bit. Enough." He set the plates down and grabbed a knife from the drawer. "It is bad to understand."

"You mean 'hard to understand'," Danielle remarked. "That's why I'm here—to get you to where it is easy to understand, make sure you know some of our slang."

He wrinkled his brow, and Danielle reached into the dusty leather bag to pull out several resources. He looked at her and pushed them away.

"No, you teach," he said, pointing to her. "Libri, no."

Danielle sighed and pointed to Portia. " 'Cane'?"

"Si," he said.

"Inglese, 'dog'."

She petted Portia after the lab walked over to her. She smiled and leaned forward, and Portia licked her.

Chudamani sat down and palm-planted his forehead. The woman was an animal lover and a fashion murderer.

"Dov'è il tuo amico?"

"Fiorella is on her way. She had to run to get some things from my apartment."

"Perché?" He raised his brow at her.

Danielle reached her to her bag and pulled out the contract and terms of what she had to do within a year. She gave another copy to him, and he looked at her. The Italian-English treaty was about to get intense. His hazel gaze skimmed through the contract and stopped at: *"Translator will have full access to client, will learn their everyday routine and translate what they do in the English language to help the client fully emerge into a new culture."*

"Di merda!" He cursed and stood up. "No...you cannot live here!"

"According to my contract, I have too."

"No, personal."

"It wouldn't be the first time I lived with a man before."

"Che?"

"Nothing, long time ago. I have too."

He shook his head and walked to the door. He pointed to it, and she folded her arms.

"Contract," she said.

"Out." He pointed to the door.

"Contract." She stared at him.

He walked over, grabbed both contracts, and threw them in the oven. He turned it on, and she rushed over to pull it out before it got started. He grabbed it again and tossed it in.

"No!" Danielle shouted.

"Si!" He snapped back.

"No!"

He pulled the contract from her and used the gas stove.

"You are crazy; do you understand?"

"No."

"You do understand; you're a psychopathic man!" Danielle shouted at him.

The two of them began to shout at each other in their own native tongues. Danielle felt as if the Italian singer was intentionally trying to sabotage everything. She threw her arms in the air, and he continued to rant about how he did not need her.

"Really? Well, good luck." Danielle stared at him. "You have no respect for anyone but yourself. You are selfish and full of yourself. Pompous asshole."

She flopped down on the chair and stared at him, while he remained standing. The language barrier was not the issue—it was the thick-skulled man who refused to try.

"What are you scared of?"

He stared at her, as he did not understand what she was asking.

Danielle sighed. "Cosa hai paura di?"

"No," he said and shook his head.

She rolled her eyes, removed her dark framed glasses, and rubbed her head. He looked at her, while she just massaged her temple. There was something she and he had in common with one another, and he reached into the top cabinet to pull out a pill bottle.

He shook it and sat it on the table. Danielle stared at the familiar label. She reached for it and took two white extra strengths. Her sharp, blue-eyed gaze looked at him, and he pointed to his head.

"Migraines?" She questioned.

"Si. Migraines," he answered clearly.

She slid the bottle of pills back, and he took two before one came on, despite the twitch of annoyance that was sitting at his table. He sat down and pulled the contract.

"Two months," he stated. "I give you two months."

"I have to do a year." Danielle rubbed her head.

He reached for paper and began to write something down. She wrinkled her brow, as she noticed he was writing in English.

"I can work with this. Just need to teach you sentence formation." She looked at the paper.

Portia began to bark before someone knocked on the door. Chudamani walked over and peered through the peephole. He opened the door and looked at the Italian woman who chewed him out the other day for spilling coffee on her friend.

"Chudamani," she casual said. "Danielle, how did you teach the monkey to open the door?"

"Vaffanculo," he spat.

"Charming." Fiorella walked over and sat Danielle's stuff on his sofa. "I brought what I could in two bags, but I can go later."

"Thank you, Fiorella." Danielle looked over.

She smiled and looked at Chudamani, who folded his arms. Fiorella danced around Portia, and he began to laugh at her. She narrowed her eyes at him as she shooed Portia away.

"Dogs are not my thing," Fiorella mentioned. "So, do I need to bring a lint brush too?"

"No, I'm fine." Danielle looked at Portia, as the lab had found her way back to her. "Such a sweet little baby."

"You do have away with animals." Fiorella directed her comment to Chudamani.

He flipped her off and pointed to the contract. She walked over and skimmed the multi-chaptered contract. She explained, in detail, that he had to abide by the contract, or else he'd lose his deal with the label. She folded her arms, and he gave a groan.

"So, can you teach the old man how to speak on command?" Fiorella questioned.

"He's great at writing English, but his speaking is not so good. I can get him to speak in three months. That's why I was hired." Danielle looked at Chudamani.

She was trying to be positive on helping him clean up his English, but there was going to be push back from the fifty-something-year-old. He was not willing to bend over and take it from the label; he was going to be a rebel until it came down to the last second. She couldn't explain how many people in businesses welcomed new tours in a foreign city, but Chudamani didn't.

"He's a hold-out." Fiorella reached into the bag of pastries. "You got the ones from the café at the corner. I've been wanting to get some, but there's always a line by the time I get up."

"You mean ten o'clock."

"I got to keep my youth. You Americans get up too early to work a twelve-hour day. I like to go on a set, flash my smile, then walk off to sleep."

"Pigro!" Chudamani mentioned.

"I am lazy, and I keep my youth. Unlike you— looking all wrinkly like you just got out the shower."

"Fiorella, not helping." Danielle rubbed her head.

She stood up and looked at her friend who helped her adjust to Italian lifestyle. She didn't judge her for the way she looked or dressed. It was the best friendship she could ever wish for while trying to find a place that was laid back.

"I'm sorry." Fiorella munched happily on the pastry, which she claimed she could not really have as an aspiring Italian actress and model. "So good."

"Fiorella."

"I promise, I'll diet after this one."

"Not what I was going to say, but ok. Could you give me a minute?"

"Sure. Oh, by the way, his neighbors are very curious about the American woman who was invited into his apartment. I'd keep it down, you two." Fiorella winked. "Don't want them to get an idea about why their adorable Chudamani is inviting a strange woman into his apartment."

She walked towards the door and pulled her phone out.

"I'll go grocery shopping for you two. Have a chat." Fiorella walked out the door and quickly closed it before Portia got out.

The lab walked over and laid by Chudamani's feet, who took several deep breaths. Danielle watched as the struggling fifty-something-year-old stared at her.

"I think it's going to be a long day," She muttered.

"Si."

That afternoon, Danielle found silence walking along the city streets. The inhabitants watched her and whispered about where she came from. She knew they would get use to her eventually; they just didn't trust new people.

Her unique style of fashion also drew some snickering from the youth of the small town. She didn't very much care, though, and walked along the cobble-stoned streets until she reached a café. She walked into the quiet café and ordered coffee and a pastry.

"You are the strange American girl that just arrived here," a youthful voice mentioned.

She glanced up at the dark-haired young man. His eyes were the color of chocolate, and his olive complexion was perfect for someone of his age.

"Yes, I'm the strange American girl." She smiled. "I'm a translator."

"Ah, are you friends with Chudamani, or are you his new lover?" The young man asked.

Danielle laughed a little. He couldn't possibly be serious about her being his lover. She sat her phone down and stared at the youth.

"No, he's my boss."

"Boss? Chudamani is a boss of someone. No, you must be pulling my leg."

"No, I'm serious. He pays me to teach him English. I'll be around a lot, trying to help him. He's planning to tour the States soon. His willingness to impress the Americans is quite impressive."

The young man smiled at her. "You are very pretty, signora. I'd be careful around him. He tends to let his hands travel. I love him like an uncle, but he's definitely a little grabby for an old man."

"Thanks for the warning." Danielle laughed.

"I'm Stefano; I'm the son of the owner. My father is Tito, a very business-oriented man." Stefano smiled. "Let me know if you need anything else, signora."

"Grazie, Stefano." She smiled at the youth.

Her gaze fell to the articles on Chudamani. He was a man of integrity and a good friend to the churches around the Roman parishes. He had charities that supported mothers in crisis and widows of armed forces of Italy. At some point, he lost his footing in the music industry and just recently reappeared.

"Buon pomeriggio, signora," Chudamani's voice came from behind.

She turned and looked at the Italian. He was dressed as if he were about to run a marathon. She pointed to his attire, and he shrugged.

"I run. Clears my mind." His broken English was noticeable.

"I used to do the same." She smiled. "Would you like to join me?"

"Si." He pulled the chair out and sat across from her.

"So, your brother's a priest?"

"Si, he teaches in Roma."

"Preaches?"

"Si."

"How long has he been a priest?"

"Four years in the Italian army and five years with his own parish." Chudamani looked at her.

"Nine years is amazing, especially serving in the army."

Chudamani looked at her, as she scrolled through her phone.

"Why do you wear the colors?" He asked.

"What?"

"The bright colors. The weird clothes, too." He pointed at her attire. "It is blinding."

"I like color." She smiled. "It makes me happy."

"You have no sense."

"What?"

"No fashion senses. You…uh…strut with no guidance." Chudamani stared at her.

Danielle looked at him and pointed to the bland colors he wore.

"You wear dull colors—whites, blacks, browns—with the occasional pale colors," she mentioned.

"I am Italian; we dress to suit the city we live in." Chudamani looked at her. "I see no reason to dress like a peacock. And I would never."

Danielle leaned back in her chair and shook her head. She hated dull colors and remained in defense of her colorful attire.

"I make a statement."

"You make a rainbow cry."

She sipped her coffee and stood up, throwing a Euro down.

"Grazie, Stafano!" She looked at him and shook her head.

Danielle stepped out into the brisk Italian air and pulled at the knit, red scarf. She walked down the street and watched as the afternoon welcomed the children back to school and the shops to reopen.

"You are offended so easily," Chudamani stated.

"I'm offended, yes, but because you are so blunt about stupid things. And suddenly I feel you have been able to speak English all this time."

"Broken English," he said.

"Liar. Why am I really working with you?" Danielle asked.

"Label."

"No, that's not it."

Danielle glanced at the spectators, who watched the American and Italian bicker at each other. She looked back at him and brushed past him.

"I'm going to call someone to clear things up."

"Because I don't like being told what to do, so I'm being punished. They want me go to another country to find my voice." He stomped his foot.

Danielle glanced at him and wrinkled her brow.

"I haven't had a hit in two years. They think I lost my spirit and that going to another country will spark some inspiration."

She walked back over and raised her brow at him. He stared down at her five-foot-four-inch figure, towering over her. She pursed her lips and glanced around as they still were being watched.

"I'm supposed to help save your career; that's just perfect. The little, strange American girl is to help the tall, egoistical Italian singer."

"That's not fair."

"Isn't it? You insult my clothes and who knows what else." Danielle stood straight and let her foot drag back and forth on the cobble stone street. "So, let's find your voice."

Chudamani looked at her, as her petite figure remained standing.

"Partners?" Chudamani stuck his hand out to her.

"Partners." Danielle looked at him and grabbed his hand to shake.

He smirked and pulled her to him, kissing her on the lips. The spectators around them cheered and clapped.

She pulled away and slapped him across the face, before walking in the other direction. He chuckled and took a bow, announcing that he still had it.

CHAPTER THREE

The days that they started to work were scheduled between his up and coming shows in Rome. He had six shows around the ancient city, then another three in surrounding areas. His popularity as one of the greats dwindled in certain circles around the area. There was chatter amongst his own circles that maybe stepping out of limelight was what would be best—let them miss him, and then have the great comeback.

Danielle watched endless rehearsals, and she criticized them for her own personal enjoyment. She teased him for his overdone sets and chats with the audience.

"You are just a translator," he would state in annoyance.

"I may be a translator, but I know shows." Danielle would get up on stage.

"This is not your world, signora."

Fiorella and Antonio would watch as the two snapped at each other.

"They are like this all the time," Fiorella muttered. "I just don't get why they don't sleep together and get it over with. He surely wants to sleep with Danielle; look at his body language."

"Chudamani's not desperate, signora, but I do see the tension between the two." Antonio glanced at her.

"Trust me, I know when a man wants to sleep with a woman. I've had my fair share. And maybe the two of them should, release the stress from both sides."

Antonio shook his head and walked onstage to break up the fighting. Danielle stomped her foot in aggravation and walked off the stage, as Antonio took over.

"He's so stubborn!" Danielle snapped. "And infuriating!"

"Don't come on my stage! This isn't your business!"
He yelled back at her.

"I wouldn't if you did things right!"

"Easy. Take a walk, Danielle. He's not going to
change anytime soon." Antonio gave her shoulder a pat. "Let
me speak with Chudamani and see what I can do."

Danielle breathed, grabbed her black, wool coat, and
she walked out into the sunny day, pulling the coat tightly
around her. She stormed out, passing a young priest heading
in the opposite direction.

"Scusa, signora," the priest said.

"Si?"

"Sto cercando Chudamani Amoretto.

"He's in there blowing steam out." She pointed to
stage door.

"Oh, you're his American companion."

Danielle looked at the clean-cut younger man and
realized that he was Chudamani's brother. She apologized
for her temper, and he chuckled.

"How about a walk?" He asked.

"Don't you need to speak to him?"

"I think letting him cool off is best, and it looks like
you could use a friend." The younger brother smiled.

Danielle nodded, and he walked with her. He guided
her towards a café, which was a popular place to see the
Roman celebrities who resided in the ancient city.

"My brother is hard to deal with sometimes,"
Chudamani's brother commented.

"A little? I barely can get one sentence in before he
blows me off." Danielle looked at him. "He said that the
label said he has lost his voice. What does that mean?"

Chudamani's brother lifted the hot beverage and
looked at the young American woman.

"He's lost his path in many ways. Music,
spirituality—the list is long. He used to be a devout Catholic.
Every Sunday, rain or shine, he'd be at my church. It's hard

to believe, in a six-month period, he's lost the sense of being. Chudamani cares deeply for the life he lives but forgets his other needs. I believe, despite the toughness he faces, he prevails with the help of God. Of course, I'm a priest, so I have to believe that God is working hard on him."

"What happened six months ago?" Danielle asked.

"He was left at the altar. His fiancée ran off with a younger man. I was to marry them, and they were on track, but, when the music played, she did not walk down the aisle. I saw my brother's spirit break that day. She disappeared from his life, and he packed up all his belongings and moved out of the city. His music died with a part of his soul. He's sworn off being in love and sworn off believing that God has plans for him."

Danielle listened to the thirty-nine-year-old priest talk about his older brother. She was trying to figure out how her job could help his future in the career.

"Danielle, is it?"

"Yes," she answered.

"I believe that, in time, his wounds will heal. But what you are doing for him may be what he's needs—to feel alive again. He argues with people just to feel that he still has that vigor, and I get the impression you are the same. Your sense of style showcases a very cheery young woman, and your aggravation is for all the right reasons, but don't let him irritate you."

Danielle smiled a little, and the young priest reached for some money. She stopped him and placed a couple of Euros.

"What can I do to help?" Danielle asked.

"Just wait. He will come to you when the time is right. Let him believe he is in control, Danielle. He needs to feel that right now. He's stubborn man, but he is loved."

Danielle glanced at the scars on his hands and wrinkled her brow at them.

"He said you served in the Italian army," Danielle said.

"I did. Four years of hard service. I was wounded in the field giving the last sacrament to a dying soldier. I believe God wanted me here in Rome to grow his church. This parish was small, and now a flock of very devout Catholics have come home. My hands are limited to motion, but, in serving God, I work as a reminder that He works in mysterious ways."

"I am sure Chudamani is proud of your service, both as a former solider of war and a solider of God."

"He was there when I took my vows. It was Chudamani who encouraged me to follow my calling, deny what our parents had. Like St. Francis of Assis, I gave up my worldly possessions and became a priest. My father and mother were disappointed, but I was alright. And Chudamani comes to visit; he's the only family that still talks to me. He's a good person, Danielle, and I think you see that."

"It just seemed like, three days ago, he decided to pull a fast one."

"What do you mean?"

"He kissed me in front of the town. I did have to put him in his place and slap him…couldn't forgive that."

His brother laughed and shook his head.

"That is my brother—always on for a show. Did they clap?"

"Of course."

"I will speak with him on that."

"Danielle!" Chudamani called. "I need you!"

"And I supposed this ends our conversation, Father."

"Call me Francis." The younger brother extended his hand.

"A pleasure to meet you, Francis." Danielle shook his hand.

"I'll be around," Francis said.

She grabbed her purse and rushed over to the impatient man. She rolled her shoulders back and stared at him, as he stood there.

"What do you need?" Danielle asked.

"I need your help with some phrasing." Chudamani pointed to the white index cards.

She looked at the fifty-something-year-old man; he seemed too relaxed. She continued to look at him, while his foot tapped.

"Did you take something?" She asked, as her brow wrinkled at him.

She leaned forward and sniffed the air around him. She slapped him on the arm, and he looked at her, jerking back.

"You're fucking high!"

"Ouch! I'm not high; I'm relaxed."

"You idiot!" She slapped him again.

She shook her head, snatched the cards from him, and walked to the venue. He chased after her and tried to convince her that he didn't smoke anything. She ignored him, becoming stressed.

"Why were you talking to my brother?" Chudamani asked.

"None of your business."

"What did he say?"

"You need to chill the fuck out, Chudamani."

"You need to lower your voice."

Danielle looked at Fiorella and walked over to her.

"What did you give him?"

"What didn't I give him?" Fiorella laughed.

"I'm gone for five minutes, and you give him drugs."

Fiorella laughed and handed her a joint.

"Fresh. He wasn't supposed to inhale." She covered her mouth.

"No, I don't do that." Danielle walked over to his stage crew and told them to get lunch. "Chudamani, you need to chill out."

He looked at her, as he sat down on the stage. She joined him and cupped his face in her hands, and he smiled at her.

"Your eyes are really blue," he said.

"I know. Did you drink anything?"

She looked over at Fiorella, who chuckled. Danielle shook her head and hoped he didn't have too much. He was too loose, and she didn't like the idea that his manager would be back.

"Hey, get me some water," she told a stage member.

"Why don't you want to help me?" He asked, swaying a little.

Fiorella walked over with a bottle water, and Danielle opened it. She handed it to him, and he grabbed her hand to bring the bottle to his lips.

"Seriously, how much did you smoke?" She gave him a look of annoyance.

"Enough to totally feel it." Fiorella laughed.

Danielle sighed, and Chudamani gave a dopy smile. He lightly reached up and pushed a fallen lock of her auburn hair.

"You dress funny."

"Ok, that's it! Time to get up and move around." She pushed herself up.

She stood up and put out her hand to him. He grabbed it and got up with wabbly footing. She grabbed hold of him by his tight jean's pocket before he fell forward, and he stepped back to gain his footing. Her hands hovered around to make sure he didn't go too far one way or the other.

"Food is here!" Antonio called.

"Great! Let's get him food. Fiorella, don't do that again."

Fiorella laughed a little, and Danielle knew she did it on purpose. She enjoyed seeing Chudamani in a fog.

As the fog wore off, Chudamani laid down with a cloth on his head. He was moaning in his dressing room, while Danielle stood and watched him.

"Your crazy friend drugged me." He covered his eyes from the lights.

"Do you need anything?"

"Stop the room from spinning. The last time I was that high was back in college. My brother and I use to smoke behind the university building. We smoked some hard stuff." Chudamani sat up.

"You let your priest brother smoke? You are going to hell!" Danielle was wide eyed at the story.

"No, he wasn't a man of God yet. Spawn of Satan, maybe. It was before he got 'the calling'.

She walked over and sat down beside him, handing him the cloth, which he placed on his forehead. She glanced around the dressing room and stared at the rosery hanging on the mirror along with other spiritual items.

"Your brother told me you lost your way, but I think there are signs that you didn't," she said.

He glanced up at her, and she pointed to the religious items. His hazel colored eyes went soft, and he got up, slightly stumbling before regaining his footing. He picked up the wooden rosery and stared at it.

"You don't just throw away these things. I don't believe they help me, but there is a comfort that comes from having them around. My brother gave me the rosery after he took his vows. It was a gift for my persistence that he was much more devout than I was." Chudamani placed it back onto the nail in the wall.

He rubbed his head and once more and sat down. Danielle reached over and handed him another bottle of water.

"You have got to find a new look; those colors are messing with my head," Chudamani said. "Especially right now…I still feel high, and I'm hungry again."

Danielle laughed a little and stood up, as she stared at the loud-colored skirt. She liked the mosaic pattern and the boots she wore with it.

"There's nothing wrong with my style." Danielle turned to him.

"Italy is weeping when you walk down the street in that getup." Chudamani pointed.

"Fine. Let's make a deal."

He gargled the water and swallowed it, before looking at her.

"You change your style a little—colors, I mean—and I'll tone mine down." Danielle looked at him with her right auburn brow raised. He took a deep breath and glanced at her up and down.

"Deal. But I don't want crazy colors like that," He pointed out.

"You made a deal."

"I don't want to look like a bumble bee with stripes. Solid colors and nothing that will call attention to me."

Danielle smiled and walked over to him. He looked up at her with unease, and she leaned forward and kissed his head like a mother would her son.

"I hate that, by the way."

"I call it pay back for what happened in the piazza." She smiled.

###

The venue was filled with both long-time fans and newly inspired ones, while Chudamani warmed up his vocals in his dressing room. He stared at himself in the mirror to give the pep talk he always gave himself before each show. His hazel eyes were filled with hope that no problems would happen.

He walked to a wall and leaned against it before sliding down to the cold floor. He closed his eyes, listening to sounds around him. His hands clasped together, as he found a moment of peace to focus on his breathing, humming the opening song as he cleared his head.

"I am going to get through it," he recited to himself.

There was a knock on the door, and he opened one eye to stare at it. No one said anything, so he closed his eye again and pressed his hands together. He recited once again and found his center, ignoring the silence that the intruder of his peace left.

"Chudamani," Danielle's voice came.

He opened one eye and stared at the door. "I'm in meditation, go away."

Chudamani closed his eye again.

"Chudamani, I need to go over something with you," Danielle said.

He moaned and grinded his teeth. He stood up, walked briskly to the metal door, and swung it open to see Danielle standing with the opening act. He bit his tongue to stare at the young women, who seemed nervous about going on stage.

"Come." He gestured for them to come in.

He looked at Danielle as she smiled. He took selfies with the young starlets, who adored him and aspired to reach the top of the charts like he did.

"My mother really loves you," one girl said.

"Does she? Is she pretty?" Chudamani asked.

"She's divorced," The girl said. "Can you take a picture with just me, so I can send it to her?"

"Of course." Chudamani stood by the girl and took a picture.

They squealed with joy, and Danielle shook her head. She shuffled them out and turned back to find him looking at her.

"That's the shit I'm talking about," Chudamani said. "The recent winners for the latest crazed show. Can't get a deal on their own."

Danielle shut the door and looked at him with a serious look on her face.

"Couldn't wait to ask that question, could you?" Danielle asked.

"Of course not. I'm not married. I can flirt with whomever I want to."

"You better go to confession tomorrow, then, if you're going to sleep with one of those girls who are three-times younger than you."

He shook his head and shuffled her out of his dressing room. He locked the door and returned to find peace before he was going on stage.

Chudamani finally made his way down the hall of the stadium and stretched his arms. He lifted his ear piece and did a check. Danielle looked at him in his tight jeans and untucked white shirt, and then she glanced over at his manager, as he dictated what happened when Chudamani took a break.

"Scusa," a masculine voice came behind her.

She turned around and stared a gentleman in a t-shirt and jeans, who looked about Chudamani's age. He walked towards the edge of stage, lifting an ear piece into his ear. She bit her lip, knowing exactly who stood beside her.

"Vicenzo!" Antonio greeted the man that stood beside her.

He greeted the manager with a tight handshake, before he glanced over at Danielle and smiled.

"Vicenzo, this is Danelle; she is Chudamani's assistant. She's American and knows how to choke up on the reigns." Antonio put his arm around Danielle. "Danielle, this Vicenzo—"

"Scordato. I'm familiar with your music. It's an honor to meet you." Danielle extended her hand, trying not to get overexcited.

"Ah, you are impressive, signora." Vicenzo shook her hand. "And your style—I see you love colors."

Antonio chuckled and looked at Chudamani, as he was rocking it out.

"How's he doing out there?" Vicenzo asked.

"Killing it, obviously," Antonio replied.

"I got worried when he cancelled an appearance last time. I thought it was his lungs again."

"Wait, what about his lungs?" Danielle asked.

"Nothing, signora. He just had a cold." Antonio made a quick cover up. "He's got the best vocal coach in Italy."

Vicenzo looked at the young woman and smiled. "Nothing to worry about. So, when am I going out there?"

"Any minute. He wanted to get the crowd up and out their seats, before they would storm the stage when you come on."

"Bene, bene. We're going to blow their minds tonight!" Vicenzo rolled his shoulders back.

The show was on fire when Vicenzo Scordato came on. The two close friends, both in the industry and off stage, added fire and comedic banter on stage. Danielle watched the two of them as they rushed the front of the stage and interacted with the fans.

"Ah, I know that look," the manager said.

"What look?"

"The gaze of 'maybe Chudamani isn't an asshole after all'." Antonio leaned against the back-up speakers. "Yes, at least one woman who meets Chudamani Amoretto falls for the old bastard. They fight it at first, but then submit to how they feel."

Danielle looked at him and shook her head. She folded his arms and stared at the older singer. She would never, and, plus, she wasn't his type. He dated models and famous women. She was a lowly translator from the States.

"Alright, he's coming off the stage to do a quick change." Antonio shuffled stagehands around.

"Vicenzo Scordato!" Chudamani shouted as he stepped back for Vicenzo to take a bow.

"Chudamani Amoretto!" Vicenzo applauded his friend.

Both walked off stage and removed their earpieces. The stagehands handed them bottles of water while they walked down the hall.

They walked to the dressing room and took a load off.

"So, the dame that follows you around, where did your label find her?" Vicenzo asked.

"She's the translator who is supposed to help me break into the States market, be an international sensation." Chudamani wiped his face.

"She's young and cute, despite those clothes." Vicenzo leaned back to feel the cool air brush his damp face.

Chudamani threw his towel at him, and Vicenzo laughed.

"You're still a man, aren't you?" Vicenzo teased. "Have a little fun; then, she'll get to blab to her friends that she slept with a real man."

Chudamani shook his head, as he got up to wipe the dripping sweat.

"How long has it been?"

"Since what?" Chudamani looked at his friend while using the mirror.

"You know."

"Five months."

"No, shit!" Vicenzo said with complete shock. "Chudamani, it is time to get back on that horse and ride."

He shook his head and poured water over it.

"And she's your training horse. You have the perfect set up. She's not super pretty, but she's decent."

"It's not happening." Chudamani turned and looked at Vicenzo. "I've sworn off that…Tazia broke me."

Vicenzo stood, walked over Chudamani, and gave his shoulder a pat.

"Just think about it." Vicenzo walked out and headed towards the stage.

Chudamani went to the back and reached for a fresh shirt. He wiped down his upper body, before slipping the fresh, pressed shirt on. He glanced in the mirror and stared at his reflection. He had no reason to try to find what he needed outside his career—he already believed love would never find him again. He wore the scars, instead, and used them in his music.

A sudden knock pulled him from his thoughts, and he looked over.

"Chudamani, it's time to finish," Danielle's voice said from the other side of the door.

"Be there in two minutes."

"Okay."

Hearing the heels of her boots step away, he looked in the mirror and brushed his hands over the stubble of hair. He pushed off the counter and walked towards the door. It was time to finish strong.

###

Danielle waited for Chudamani while he finished cleaning up. She walked out on the stage, as they cleared it for the evening, and sat at the edge of it. Her eyes stared out into where the audience had just occupied the seats, and she listened to the silence.

Chudamani walked out of the dressing room and walked down the halls. He was congratulated for a job well done while he walked on towards the stage. He saw Danielle sitting there, and he could only think about what Vicenzo said about getting back on the horse, but he wasn't interested in even attempting it again. His hazel eyes looked down at his hands to stare at the scar on his left. It was just a dot, but it reminded him of a different time.

"Great show, Chudamani," his guitar player said as he patted him on the shoulder.

"Thanks," he said, returning the pat. "See you tomorrow."

"You bet! I think Natalia is coming tomorrow, maybe Vicenzo again too."

"Great! It's always a party with the three of us get together!" Chudamani smiled at the idea that his closest musician friends would join him onstage.

He took a deep breath and walked up to Danielle.

"Hey, ready to go?" Chudamani asked, as he slipped the knit sock hat on.

"Yeah, I didn't know if you feel up to it, but Fiorella asked me if you'd like to do post drinks?"

"Ah, not a good idea. I just took migraine medicine. But you go ahead; I'll leave a key under the mat for you."

"Great!" Danielle got up and called a car for the two of them. "I guess tomorrow we'll work on presentation."

"Always ready to learn." He smiled.

"Great." Danielle smiled.

They walked out into the brisk weather, and Chudamani walked her to one car. He opened the door for her, and she slid in.

"Hey, how about living up to that deal and taking the train to visit Vicenzo's wife's shop? She's got all kinds of things that may be suitable for you."

"And what about you?" Danielle looked at him.

"I'll figure it out." He smiled.

"Ok, we'll talk."

He nodded, shut the door, and watched as the car pulled away from the curb. Stuffing his hands into his pockets, he looked at his driver.

"I think I'll walk. If I need a ride, I'll call you," Chudamani said.

The driver nodded, as Chudamani walked down the street. He looked up at the sky; it was clear as the Roman streets. He zipped up his coat, before he breathed into his chilled hands. The Italian fall was cooler than most, or maybe he found his current mindset made it so.

As he walked, he stopped and listened to the ten o'clock chimes from the church. He walked about half a block and saw his brother closing the church up.

"Francis," Chudamani called.

Francis glanced up and gave a wave. Chudamani walked over, and his brother hugged him before giving him a pat on the cheek.

"I would have come tonight, but I had a couple of confessions that took longer than I thought," Francis said. "How was your show?"

"It was good. Can I buy you a cup of coffee?"

"Come with me to the rectory; I'll put a fresh pot on." Francis smiled.

They walked a few feet and went through a gate to where there was a small apartment. Francis opened the door and welcomed his brother in, before walking to the small kitchen.

"This is cozy," Chudamani said.

"It is when all you need is the bare minimum." Francis put the Italian coffee pot on the stove. "So, what brings you out at this hour?"

Chudamani removed his knit sock hat and stuffed it into his jeans pocket. He rubbed his head a little, and Francis reached below for a bottle.

"I think this is maybe what you need," Francis said, holding the dark bottle of whiskey.

"Yes, the good stuff. I didn't know you could drink." Chudamani smiled.

Francis pulled two glasses down, and Chudamani poured them a glass. They lifted them up and toasted, before taking the shot.

"So, what is on your mind?" Francis asked. "I can see you are troubled."

Chudamani looked at the glass and swirled the droplets around. He lifted his hazel-gaze to meet his brother's and gave a little nod.

"Is it wrong for me to return to the dating world after six months?" Chudamani asked.

"Well, you were ditched, not widowed. But the real question is, are you ready to start down that road? Do you feel you need more time, that there is no more bad taste in your mouth? Tazia left you with a note; those scars don't heal quickly."

Chudamani slid his glass over, and Francis poured him another glass.

"This shit will put hair on your chest, brother." Chudamani wrinkled up his face as he down the liquid of sin. He hissed through a grimace, "Sorry."

"It isn't like I haven't heard those words before, but I'd curve the tongue."

"I know. It's just that you are my brother, and I still see the dorky little brother I use to chase up the creepy trees mom had planted to make the house look nicer."

Francis laughed, as the two brothers began to share their war stories from growing up. The idea of going back into the dating world had been drowned out by the laughter of memories. They couldn't ignore how time had ticked away into the early hours.

"Chudamani, maybe you need to talk to whoever you are thinking about. See how they feel and respect their decision." Francis walked him to the door. "And come to mass. Maybe there is something God can help you with."

Chudamani turned and looked at his little brother. He reached over and hugged him, before walking out.

"Mass isn't what I need."

"Lust isn't either, and I know you, brother." Francis stood at the door. "Church, Sunday, listen for the bells."

"Good night!" Chudamani said.

"I'll pray for you!"

"You do that!"

Chudamani walked on and listened for the evening celebrations of night clubs, prostitutes, and booze. He walked towards the bus station and sat down, leaning forward and moaning a little. He had forgotten about his migraine medicine, and he still decided to drink.

"God help me," he muttered.

He lifted his gaze to the sound of the city bus squealing to a halt. He reached into his pocket and pulled out his bus card, before climbing on.

"Buonasera," the bus driver welcomed him.

"Buonasera." He swiped his card.

The card reader beeped out of error, and he tried it again.

"I swear I refilled this." He tried again.

"Here, allow me," a delicate voice came.

The young woman reached over and swiped her card twice. He looked over at her to thank her, and she smiled. He walked to the back and had a seat.

"Tough night?" the delicate voice woman asked.

"A rather interesting turn of events." Chudamani looked at the beautiful Italian woman. "And you?"

She smiled and pulled from her dress a roll of cash. He gave a chuckle, and she stuffed it back into the sequined dress. She looked at him and eyed him.

"Still early," she said.

"I'm ok. I have someone waiting for me at home." Chudamani turned the woman down.

"Your wife doesn't need to know. A real quick one before you get off?"

Chudamani looked at her and shook his head.

"Appreciated, but she would know, and I would know. Very loyal to my wife, even when we fight."

"You're a good man," she said. "Unlike most of clients. They would rather cheat on their wives, than make love to them."

Chudamani looked at her, and he shook his head.

"And it doesn't help that my brother is a priest," Chudamani remarked.

"Oh, what church?"

"Santa Anna."

"Oh, I love Padre Francis! Confession every Saturday afternoon, five days a week." She smiled.

Chudamani looked at the young woman, who often lived in a sinful life and still found time for a higher power.

"This is my stop." He pointed. "Have a nice night."

"You too."

The bus stopped, and he called for a car. The late-night ride was an experience that he couldn't help but feel inspired by for new music.

He pulled out his phone and made notes of what he was going to do. Perhaps there was good coming his way, something he just needed inspiration for.

CHAPTER FOUR

The following day, the sound of someone pounding on the door woke Portia up, which woke him up. He moaned and rolled out of bed, grabbing only pants this time. He walked to the door and looked through the peephole.

He opened the door and looked at Danielle, who was carrying the loud-colored shoes in one hand and her coat in the other hand.

"Walk of shame looks good on you," Chudamani mentioned.

Danielle flipped him off and walked into the house. She patted Portia and flopped on the couch.

"I'll make you a hangover remedy," he sighed.

He walked to the small kitchen and began to mix up what he knew as a 'great' remedy. He looked over and saw that Danielle crashed, and Portia was pawing at her. He walked over and pulled the blanket over her.

"Could only image how she got back." Chudamani looked at Portia.

In the late morning, Danielle woke up, and there was a note next to a cup on the coffee table. Portia rested peacefully on the other side of the sofa, waiting for her to wake up.

She reached for the note that read: *Went for a run. Clean up and I'll introduce you to my stylist.* She stared at the brown liquid that sat in the cup. Her nose wrinkled, but she grabbed it anyways. She sniffed it and gaged, before drinking the unsatisfying-appearing drink.

Danielle grabbed her shoes and walked to the spare bedroom, which was stocked with records from decades of music. She pulled out fresh clothes, before stumbling to the shower. She turned the water on and leaned against the wall, waiting for it to run warm. Her head pounded, and she was hoping that, before they left, she would be a little more decent appearing.

Chudamani finally came in from his run, and Portia braked at him. He removed his earphones and looked at the six-year-old lab. She wagged her tail, and he took a seat to breathe.

"Hey, my girl." He rubbed her ears and kissed her head. "Did you take care of the patient?"

Portia barked, and he smiled, before reaching into fridge to grab a bottle of cold water. He looked at the empty glass from his hangover cure and smiled, lifting the glass to stared at the pink residue that remained as he sighed.

It was then that the bathroom door opened, and he leaned to the side to see if Danielle was getting out.

"Danielle," he called.

"Yes?"

"I'm just letting you know I'm here," Chudamani called.

"Great, could you look away?"

"Are you naked?"

"No," she called back.

"Oh…then, yes, I can."

"Asshole."

He chuckled and looked at Portia, as she blinked at him. He wrinkled his brow and turned away to use the microwave's reflective surface to look out into the living area. Portia growled at him, and he looked at her.

"Harmless peek," Chudamani muttered to her. "Mind your business."

She groaned and laid on the ground.

"Your judgement is not needed here."

Danielle peeked around the corner and saw his back turned. She dashed to her room and quickly pushed the door shut.

"You can turn around," Danielle called from her room.

"Good, I was starting to wonder if I was punished." He looked over at her door and saw it didn't shut all the way.

He glanced at Portia and casually walked towards it, but then there was the sudden growl that came from the six-year-old. He looked back at her, and she barked at him.

"Come on, just a peek?"

She barked again, and he pouted, mumbling about what was the point of having a female roommate if he couldn't act on his guy-instinct to peek.

"Come on, we're going be late. She's expecting us." He rubbed his head.

Portia barked at him, and he looked at her.

"It's a migraine; don't get upset." He smiled at her.

She barked at him and pawed his foot. He reached over and petted her, as he leaned forward to look into Danielle's room.

"Ok, I'm ready." Danielle walked out with a high-low skirt on and a lime-green top.

"Great, green all around." He patted his leg. "Let me hook up Portia real quick."

"Why?"

"She's coming with us today." Chudamani glanced back at her.

He reached around and pulled a harness and a vest for the lab. Danielle watched him as he stuffed a white card into his wallet and attached a clip-on license to Portia's collar.

"We're going to take the train today," he stated. "I have you covered, as I'm sure you don't get a metro card."

"I have one, but it probably needs to be filled." Danielle reached for the door.

He whistled, and Portia led the way out, followed by Danielle. He locked the door and walked with them downstairs.

The brisk fall air continued to make a statement. Chudamani zipped up his lightweight coat and pulled the hundred-and-fifty-euro sunglasses out to let them hang on his coat pocket. He glanced over at Danielle, as she remained with just a light sweater over the green outfit. He gave a sigh and led the way to the depot.

"Portia likes the shop; that's why I take her." Chudamani looked at Danielle. "She gets to ride the train and interact with the people."

They walked down towards the train depot, and he swiped his card twice, then Portia's. Both walked through the gates and Danielle petted Portia as they waited.

"Did you have a good time last night?" Chudamani asked her.

"I did. Fiorella and I went to visit good friends of hers and just celebrated." Danielle looked at him. "What did you do?"

"I just headed home and watched TV with Portia." He looked over at her

"Is that all you did?"

"What else would I do?"

"I don't know," Danielle answered.

He looked at the young woman and leaned over to pat Portia. He glanced in the distance to see the train coming their way. He stood up, and Portia barked at him.

"I'm good, girl." He gave her a pat.

"Your eyes look a little blood-shot," Danielle mentioned. "Just saying, signs of drinking."

Chudamani chuckled and slipped his sunglasses on. She looked at Portia and shrugged.

When they arrived into the Roman station, he took her to a side street just two miles from the station. Looking at the hanging sign, he opened the door.

"Gia!" He called.

"Come in, Chudamani! I'll be right with you." Gia poked her head out. "Oh, Portia, you came too!"

Chudamani undid the leash and let her greet the polished-looking woman. He looked at Danielle, who tapped her fingers on her leg. He reached over and placed his hand on top of hers.

"It'll be fine. Gia does everything I wear when I need a suit." He whispered, looking her in the eyes.

"Right, suits, not women's clothes."

"She has everything. This is Vicenzo's wife's shop. Gia is the seamstress, and Angelica is Vicenzo's wife." Chudamani continued to hold her hand. "You'll love them both."

The shop door opened, and Danielle looked over to see the receptionist from the office walk in. She wore a three-hundred-euro dress, and the sunhat that shadowed her face gave her mystery.

"Buongiorno, Gia!" Pietra called. "I've come for my dresses."

Danielle pulled her hand from Chudamani's, as she did not want rumors to circulate around the office.

"Oh, Buongiorno, Chudamani. And what a surprise to see the colorful mouse here too." Pietra smiled a little.

Chudamani stood up and both shared a peck on the cheek. "You are looking overly-prepared for the video."

"I have to look the part. I was glad you chose me over Fiorella. She's unprofessional and too in love with you." Pietra smirked.

"Most women are." He looked over at Danielle, who looked away.

He slightly frowned, and Portia came running in, barking. Pietra stepped back and nearly tripped over her heel. Chudamani grabbed her before she fell back and looked at the gorgeous woman. She smiled, removed the black hat, and grabbed his hand.

"Thank you."

Portia barked at Pietra still, and Chudamani told her to lie down. The six-year-old rushed to the back, and Danielle looked back to Pietra, who kept one hand on his arm. He still hadn't let go of her, even after she stood solid on her two feet.

"Pietra, you'll have to come back later. Angelica is adding something special to one of the dresses. She said everyone is wearing this style now and wanted to make sure yours was tailored just right." Gia stuck her head out. "Tomorrow for sure."

"Of course! I'll be here." Pietra smiled.

She turned, looked at Chudamani, and leaned forward to kiss his cheek. Her hand rushed down his back, and she placed her hand in his back pocket. Danielle's mouth dropped open slightly.

"See you real soon, Chudamani. Ciao." She waved and walked out.

"Chudamani, send your guest in. I've got to measure her." Gia stepped out.

He looked at Danielle, and she blinked. She walked quickly to the back to a smiling Gia.

"She just groped him," Danielle finally said.

"Pietra is the fairest of them all. She's also the richest. Her father was a big contributor to renovations on many things around Roma. She's so rich that she could buy a title and the house to go with it." Gia wrapped the tape measure. "She's had a huge crush on Chudamani since before she was out of diapers. She *is* his type—rich and good breeding."

Danielle looked in the mirror, as the woman measured every part of her body. She smiled and looked at her.

"But she groped him."

"She has money; he needs money." She sighed. "Might as well let the princess have her way. I wouldn't be surprised if he goes home with her after tonight."

Danielle looked at her. "Why?"

Gia stopped and looked at her, clicking her tongue. "Oh, signora, Chudamani is still a man. A woman puts the moves on him, and he's going to dive right in."

Danielle wrinkled her brow at the seamstress.

"Don't let it get to you; that's just show business." Gia stepped to the side. "Ok, Chudamani, come."

Chudamani walked to the back and looked at Danielle as she still stood there.

"What does she need?"

"Everything. Skirts, dresses, pants, tops. Blacks, whites, browns." He listed what he felt would make her fit into the Italian environment.

"I can do her hair too." Gia raised a brow.

"I have that scheduled too."

"Good for you, Chudamani. She'll need to learn to walk before you parade her to the games."

"What?"

"He's got to take you everywhere he goes. That means you are going to be on his arm at every event he attends, including concerts."

Danielle shook her head and stepped down. She grabbed his arm and pulled him away from hearing distance.

"Why are you doing this?" Danielle asked.

"Because you don't have taste."

"Then take someone who has taste. I'm just a translator. Take Pietra to the damn events. I don't need to be paraded around like some accessory to your success." She poked him in the chest. "I like how I dress. If you don't, then fuck you."

He narrowed his eyes at her, and she folded her arms. Portia barked at him and pawed at him. She tugged at his jeans, and Chudamani shooed her off him.

"Portia, that's enough!" He snapped at her. "I'm fine!"

Danielle glanced at Portia, and, before she could ask a question, she saw his eyes roll back. He collapsed onto the floor.

"Chudamani!" She cried.

Gia ran out to see Portia lay down by his head.

"Lift his head," Gia whistled.

Danielle lifted Chudamani's head, and Portia laid underneath. Gia turned him on his side and felt his body jolt. Danielle felt fear paralyze her.

"What hell?"

"He didn't tell you, did he?"

"No," Danielle looked at him.

"Talk to him, until he comes out of it." Gia got up and rushed to the back.

Danielle rubbed his back and stared at him.

"You're ok. I'm sorry." She felt his body slowly relax.

Gia walked over and lifted his hand up. She looked over at Danielle and placed a hand on her shoulder.

"Seizures," Gia said.

Danielle reached over and gently stroked his head as he blinked, and a steady breath happened. He moaned and slowly sat up. He looked at Portia as she wagged her tail. She licked his face, and he looked at Danielle.

"Gia…"

"I'll get you some water." Gia handed the towel to Danielle.

He came to his knees and placed his hand on his chest. He was quiet and reached into a pocket on Portia's vest. He pulled out the anti-seizure medicine and took two pills.

"How long?" Danielle asked.

"Twenty-four months and three weeks. I don't tell people because they look at me like I'm broken. Only a handful of people I trust with this. They started after I had a bad reaction to a treatment I had prior." Chudamani swallowed the lump in his throat. "Portia is a service dog."

Danielle stared at him, and he looked away from her. His eyes were still distant, as he hadn't fully recovered from the episode.

"I'm fine, but sometimes large amounts of stress set them off. Drinking does too…I took a year leave from my music career to get treated for them. I started meditation and running to learn to steady my breaths. The last few days have been stressful for me because of being back. I've had my doctor make my medicine stronger, so I can keep situations like this from happening.

"Here you are," Gia said, handing him the water.

"Grazie."

Danielle looked at her hands, as she was still shaking. He reached over, grabbed her hands, and rubbed them.

"How bad do they get?"

"They can get pretty violent. I've been hospitalized for them." He tried to ignore the sympathy in her eyes.

Danielle took a deep breath and reached up with the towel and wiped his face. He closed his eyes as she wiped his face with the cool towel.

"I'm sorry I didn't tell you. I just didn't know if I could trust you. The reason you're staying with me is because my label wants you to snitch on me. It has nothing to do with the States."

"Then I'll snitch," Danielle said with a shrug.

"What?"

"I have to do my job, but I won't do it until I'm ready. I can embellish with the story they want to hear." Danielle stood up and reached around to help him stand. "Partners."

He steadied his footing and looked down at her petite figure.

"Partners."

"Now, about my *real* job…I have some adjustments to make." Danielle smirked at him, and he raised his brow at her.

CHAPTER FIVE

Danielle read while Chudamani was resting. Portia remained near her master that whole afternoon, nervous after his previous episode. She set the book down and got up to quietly walk down to his room. She pushed the door open quietly, but Portia still heard and looked up at her. Danielle stepped further into the darken room; his blackout curtains kept any light from seeping in. She glanced around at the small light that came from a nightlight to give a dull illumination to see. Her eyes glanced over at him, as he slept peacefully. Her heart ached for the fifty-something-year-old; she was scared for him and his future.

"He'll be ok, girl," She whispered to the lab, continuing to look at Chudamani while he slept.

It was hard to believe that he had something wrong. He seemed normal, but there were tell-tale signs that there was something different about him. She knelt and picked up around his room quietly, putting the dirty clothes in the laundry basket.

"You don't have to pick up after me," she heard him mumble.

Danielle looked over her shoulder to see that his eyes were still closed. She walked towards his bed, and he reached out his hand to her. His hand grabbed hers.

"Could you call my brother to pick up my prescription?" He mumbled. "I called it in yesterday but forgot to pick it up.

"I can do that. What is his number?"

"It's on the cabinet where I have my medicines. You'll see it; it says dorky brother."

Danielle tried not to laugh at hearing him call his priest brother 'dorky'.

"Thank you, Danielle. You are going beyond your job title."

"You're welcome."

She walked out of his room and grabbed her phone. Pushing open the cabinet that had medicines in it, she saw Francis' number and called him.

"Ciao, Francis. This is Danielle." She sat at the kitchen table.

"Ciao, what can I do for you?"

"Chudamani asked me to call to see if you could pick up his prescription? He said it was filled yesterday."

"Of course. I'll be over in the next hour."

"Grazie."

"Prego."

She hung up and walked back to his room to hear his gentle breathing. She looked at Portia, who was now laying her head on his torso. She smiled a little, but still felt as though she needed to be close by again. She had seen him go from lively to helpless in the matter of seconds, and Danielle felt helpless alongside him. Her hands still shook remembering the sight. His eyes just rolled back, and his body became tense.

She slid down the door frame and pulled out her phone. She did a search to find out what kind of treatment he received. There was very little of anything on him after three years ago. Her eyes searched for answers, and she leaned her head on the door frame.

Portia muffed, and Danielle glanced at her. She smiled and returned looking back at her phone. Portia barked again, and he lightly patted her.

"She won't stop until you leave or come lay down." He opened his eyes.

"I can leave."

"I don't think that's what she wants." He petted her.

Danielle looked at him, and Portia moved around and got closer to him. He put his arms around her like she was a stuffed animal.

"She moved for you." He peeked one eye open at her.

"I don't think..."

"I don't bite." He moved his head to her direction to fully look at her.

Danielle smiled, stood up, and kicked off her loud-colored slippers.

"Shocker, even your slippers match your crazy outfits." He smiled.

She walked, laid down on her back, and stared up at the ceiling. She sighed and heard Portia groan. He looked over at her and rolled his eyes.

"You're so awkward."

"Aren't you supposed to be resting?" Danielle chided.

"I can't when you're being awkward."

"You're such a baby. What do you want?"

He grabbed her hand and pulled her towards him, throwing her hand around him.

"This."

She rolled her eyes and turned on her side to move close to him. To her, it became the most awkward thing.

"See? You don't have to be awkward about something so natural." He looked at her. "I'm not making a move on you."

Danielle gave him a look as she laid her head down. But before she could get comfortable, there was a knock on the door. Portia muffed, and Danielle got up to get the door before she barked.

She peeked through the peephole and saw Francis. She opened to door and told him to come in.

"Here's his prescription," Francis said.

"Thank you."

"Where is he?"

"He's resting. Portia is with him." Danielle walked to the kitchen and put a kettle on.

"So, I guess he told you."

Danielle glanced over at Chudamani's younger brother. She gave a nod and took a seat across from him.

"He had one while we were out. He had Portia, so I think he knew it was going to happen." Danielle mentioned.

"It's scary seeing this happen right in front of you. I was a mess because I did not know who he told." Francis reached over and patted her hand.

Danielle sighed and breathed a little. She felt tears swell up in her eyes and, slowly, they released, not totally sure why she was crying. Francis got up and walked over to her before sitting down.

"I don't even know why I'm crying," she wept.

"Because you were scared—this is normal. It also means you care about his wellbeing. You were in the right place at the right time. There was a reason why he had one while you were there."

"He was just lying there helpless." Danielle covered her face as she cried. "Portia was the only one who seemed to handle this like a champ."

Francis chuckled and reached for a napkin on the table. He wiped away her tears, as she worked through the emotions of experiencing someone having a seizure. It was nothing new, obviously, for his brother.

"He said he developed the seizures because of a bad reaction from a treatment. I couldn't find out what kind of treatment he had."

Francis frowned a little, and his eyes became distant.

"He had a small tumor on his left lung. It was the kind that was cancerous, and they treated him with chemo. The reaction he had caused a seizure, which put him in a coma for six months. He came out of it, slowly, and was put on an experimental treatment. His manager kept it secret, because he didn't want him to look like he couldn't keep up with the industry. When he started canceling tours and music was being delayed, they started digging and found out. They used his lack of English, which was another lie, to hide his condition until they could find someone to keep an eye on him. A 'translator'." Francis gave her a pointed look.

"We've decided I'm the snitch. I didn't even know I was a snitch. I just thought I was a simple translator."

"You are much more than a simple translator." Francis smiled. "He needs the extra eyes on him right now. If he's having seizures now, he's under stress."

Danielle sighed and wiped the tears away. She was so mean to him when she met him the first time, but he was just using his plucky personality to hide his condition.

"Will he stop having seizures ever?"

"They do eventually go away, depending on the person."

"We should cancel the show. He's so weak right now, and there's no way he can do a show." Danielle stood up to grab her phone.

"Just wait, he will rally. Plus, he's taken his anti-seizure medication." Francis put his hand on her shoulder. "Just stay close."

Danielle looked wearily at Francis with his pleading look, eventually nodding and putting her phone on the table.

"I know you made tea, but I need to go back to prepare for my sermon for Saturday afternoon and Sunday mass. Please, look out for him and, I assure you, he will be fine. When he wakes up—let him wake up a little—but give him orange juice. It will help him."

Francis stood up, and Danielle walked him to the door.

"Thank you, Francis."

"You're welcome. Perhaps, I'll see you Sunday morning. Maybe you could get him there…He needs a little help."

Danielle smiled and gave a nod. Francis never was going to give up on Chudamani to bring him back home.

"I'll see what I can do." Danielle smiled.

When Francis left, she walked back to check on Chudamani. Portia looked over at her, and he was truly asleep this time. Danielle walked over to the bed and petted Portia before leaving the room.

She curled up on the couch and, before she closed her eyes to get some sleep, she pressed the home key on her phone and then the phone icon.

"I'm sorry I couldn't catch you, but leave a message and I'll give you call back. And if you are the love of my life, you know what you have to do." The deep voice of her best friend and partner.

Danielle covered her face with the blanket. She closed her eyes and wished she was home again.

Three years ago

"Sit still, I'm almost finished," Danielle said.

Danielle painted the broad-shouldered, manly man's toes. He constantly moved his large, beaten-up feet as she brushed the hot pink nail polish on them.

"The fellas will have their suspicions when I sport this look." He leaned forward and kissed her head.

"I think it's a great color on you; it screams 'new trend'." Danielle looked up at the green-eyed, bearded man.

He came down to sit on the floor and kissed her.

"I love you, Sunshine," he said, as he pushed her hair back. "I hope this little bean will understand how colorful its mother is."

He lightly placed his hand on her stomach. She smiled and placed her hand on his.

"Or how boring its father is." She kissed his nose.

"Boring? Would a boring man let you paint his toe nails?" He grabbed ahold of her and tickled her.

She laughed as he leaned over and kissed her.

"Danielle Bennet, I love you. I love the colors you wear to keep your sunny personality. I love how you make me feel when I'm far away from you." He stroked her cheek. "I'll be home just in time to see this baby being born, and, after that, I'm only working in an office. No danger zones for me. I'll have plenty of translations to do in a boring office."

"You promise?"

"Cross my heart. We're going to be a normal family. No more government assignments. We'll start our own translation company. Go to Italy for a second honeymoon, go see those crazy singers you like."

Danielle smiled and stroked his cheek. "You better shave before you come home, because I don't want you to look like the wolfman."

"You got it! I'll have a baby-soft face."

Three years later

Danielle felt someone lightly stroke her cheek. She opened her eyes and gasped as she sat up. She looked around, and her eyes set on Chudamani as he stood above her.

"How long was I out?" Danielle asked.

"Long enough to mumble about someone named Harrison." Chudamani blinked at her.

"Oh."

He looked at her with an unnerving stare, and she pushed back her hair.

"We've got to get ready to go for the show!" She panicked when she saw the clock. "I need to change."

"Hey, hey, wait," he called.

She stopped and swallowed a lump in her throat. She looked at Portia, as the chocolate lab wagged her tail. She looked back at him and bit her lip.

"It will be alright; we pushed back the time. It's not until nine." He looked at her. "Are you sure you are okay?"

Danielle smiled and nodded. "I'm perfect."

She turned back around, and he watched her sleek off into her room. Away from him, she took a few deep breaths as she fanned away her tears. Her hands fell to her stomach, and she tried to keep her emotions out of doing her job.

He knocked, and she looked up at the closed door.

"I'm fine," she said, as she swallowed her tears.

He walked off at her answer, and she breathed a sigh of relief. It wasn't the time to explain her past when there was a future to keep moving forward.

Chudamani folded the blanket, but, as he did, her phone fell from under it. He knelt and clicked the side button, and there a soldier on her phone smiled. He looked in the direction of her room. It was none of his business, but she didn't mention anything about a boyfriend or husband.

Portia groaned, and he looked down at her.

"I just looked at the picture." He shook his head. "So judgmental."

She muffed at him, and he sat her phone on the kitchen table. He reached up in the cabinet and pulled down his medicine, leaning against the counter as he read carefully how to take the it. His doctor had once more prescribed the first medication he was on, because he had felt the new medicine kept him from participating in the life he was supposed to live.

"Alright, I'm ready." She gave a fake smile, despite how she felt.

"I'm taking my medicine. Portia is coming with us tonight." Chudamani looked up at her. "Are you sure you're ok? I'm not really keen on picking up feelings, especially right now, but I get the sense that something happened."

Danielle walked over and took a seat across from him. She saw her phone on the table and lifted it up.

"It fell on the floor when I was folding the blanket." He looked at her.

"It's fine, I guess I panicked when I thought we had to be in town." She clicked the side button to stare at the picture of the solider.

"If we're being honest, with all the things going on, may I ask who the solider is?" Chudamani asked, pointing. "I did look on your screen. I'm sorry, it's none of my business."

Danielle bit her lower lip and looked at the concern written on his face. He obviously was curious, but, he was right, it was none of his business. Of course, neither was his medical issues.

"He's my husband. I met him while I was on assignment as a translator. My husband was a solider for the U.S. Marines Corp, and he often was taking assignments overseas to help do translations. On his last tour, he was caught in enemy fire while he was trying to help a civilian mother and her six-month-old to safety before a raid happened." Danielle looked down at the picture. "That was three years ago."

"Mi dispiace, it was not my place to bring back those memories." Chudamani opened the bottle and took two pills. "Please forgive me."

"It's alright; sometimes it helps to talk about what happened. There are days I relive getting the notice. The pain comes and goes, and I took the job with the label."

"How long have you been here, Danielle?" He stood up and walked over to the chair beside her.

"Two years. I've been ok in my small office, only translating lyrics of artists to help their English-speaking fans. I did a lot of your songs before I was assigned to you, actually." Danielle looked at him. "I miss home, but I don't want to go back because I lost everything there."

She stared down at the golden ring she wore on her right hand and smiled when the black skirt she wore with the gold belt came into view.

"You are brave," Chudamani said. "I would have lost my mind."

Danielle looked up at him and placed her hand on his face.

"Bad news, Chudamani—you lost it a long time ago." She smiled as she gave his face a pat. "We need to move on and get to the show."

He gave a weak smile and looked at Portia. The chocolate lab wagged her tail and stood up, getting excited.

"Go get your vest," he whistled.

She took off through the living room. Danielle smiled and watched him as he grabbed the harness for Portia. He seemed fine, but there was a weary look still lingering in his eyes.

"Portia, come," he whistled to her.

She came running with the vest, and he slipped his medication into the pocket. He looked at Danielle and handed her the keys to the apartment. She grabbed her purse and anything else she needed.

"Will Vicenzo be joining you again?" Danielle asked, as she slipped on her coat.

"If he's free, but you'll definitely get to meet Natalia tonight."

"Natalia Laterza?"

"Yeah, we travel in the same groups. Please, don't freak out like a fan, not professional." Chudamani smiled at her.

Chudamani guided Portia out the door, and Danielle locked it tight. She followed behind Portia and Chudamani as they walked down the steps.

"Chudamani, I see you have a new roommate," the older lady from his morning commutes mentioned, carrying in her groceries.

"Let me help you, signora." Chudamani rushed to take the bags from the older woman.

"No need." She smiled and looked over at the twenty-three-year-old man next to her. "I've got a Roman god to help me."

She winked at Chudamani and handed the young man her keys.

"Bravo, you'll have to tell me how good a god is." Chudamani gave her a wink.

"And your roommate, she dresses funny, but she's very pretty. You make sure you take care of that little angel."

Chudamani laughed, as she pinched his cheek and then sent him on his way. Danielle looked at him with a raised eyebrow. He shook his head, as he remained amused by the older woman and her fantasy of the younger man.

"You do have quirky neighbors." Danielle commented.

"They just don't trust you yet. They think you are a funny American girl. You talk to everyone and are way too colorful."

"I'm from the south; we have the best hospitality," Danielle proudly stated.

He shrugged, and Portia pushed the gate open for him. He let Danielle go first and whistled for Portia to close the gate. Danielle smiled at his best friend's skill.

As they finally made it on the train, he found a spot and pointed it out to Danielle.

"No, you sit," Danielle said.

He took the seat, and Portia sat between his feet. Danielle reached for the flimsy piece of leather to hold onto. He watched, amused, as the five-foot four girl, dangled like a piece of meat on a hook.

"You sit. You look like a piece of meat dangling from a hook." He started to stand.

The train came to a harsh stop, and Danielle lost her balance. He grabbed her by her waist to keep her from flying forward and meeting a painful fall. Instead, she fell back and into his hold. Her eyes were wide from the sudden stop, but also from where her elbow had fallen.

"I'm so sorry," she apologized. "Are you ok?"

He took a deep breath and moved her elbow from the uncomfortable place. Portia sat up and licked his hand.

"I'm fine," he breathed out.

She looked at him, trying not to laugh, as his face was wrinkled like a crinkled piece of paper. She lightly patted his head and slowly stood.

"I'll be alright as soon as I regain feeling." He looked at her, seeing she was half amused by the incident, but concern also plagued her face. "Remind me never to catch you again, unless I'm prepared."

"Sorry."

"Switch spots with me and hold Portia. I'll be fine." He got up, carefully, and switched with her.

When they finally got to the venue, there were lines of fans waiting to get in. The security quickly got him in, and Danielle followed.

"Danielle," Fiorella called.

She walked over to her friend and hugged her. "Where have you been? Chudamani is half an hour late. He was supposed to rehearse. Vicenzo and Natalia were whispering backstage about hoping he was ok."

"He's fine, just missed the alarm."

"What's with the dog?" Fiorella asked.

"Bring your pet to work!" Danielle said with a nervous smile on her face. "He's fine."

Fiorella wrapped her arm around Danielle's and looked at her.

"He's fine? We're talking about Chudamani here. He's been objecting to your very presence since you started working with him. Are you ok? What drugs did he give you?"

They walked down the corridor, but Fiorella suddenly stopped her.

"Did you sleep with him?" She gasped.

"No! I did not sleep with him!" Danielle spat. "I would never!"

"I would." Fiorella smiled with a shrug.

Danielle walked towards Chudamani's dressing room and told Fiorella to stay outside. She knocked, and Vicenzo opened the door.

"Welcome, signora," he smiled. "We were just talking about how much of a help you have been."

Danielle looked at Chudamani, who shook his head.

"Don't listen to that crazy bastard. He's had a little too much." Chudamani threw an empty water bottle at Vicenzo. "Go warm your vocals; you sang off key last night."

Vicenzo smirked at him and winked as he pointed to Danielle.

"Out!" Chudamani stood up.

Danielle looked at Vicenzo, and he gave a bow as he slinked in the other direction. She walked in with Fiorella at the same time and sat down.

"Talk loudly, I'm changing," he said, as he walked into a smaller room.

"You can change out here," Fiorella mentioned.

"Fiorella."

"Look at you; you are blushing. You know you want to see his hot body," Fiorella teased. "Or have you already felt it?"

"What were you saying?" Chudamani asked.

"She wants to see your—" Danielle covered Fiorella's mouth.

"Nothing, we were just saying that your body...contract." Danielle looked at Fiorella and narrowed her eyes.

Chudamani walked out in tight, black jeans and an unbuttoned, red shirt. Danielle and Fiorella's mouths slowly dropped open. He looked at them and raised his brow.

"Ladies?"

"Could you turn around? I think there was a piece of dog hair on your pants." Fiorella smiled mischievously.

Portia groaned and walked over to Danielle. She pawed her, and Danielle shook her head.

"No," she muttered.

Portia barked at Danielle and pawed her. Danielle shook her head, and Portia curled at her feet.

"I think Portia's broken," Danielle mentioned.

He whistled, and Portia looked over at him before barking at Danielle. He looked at the two girls, as they still stared at him.

"Red too much?" He asked.

"No," Fiorella said, shaking her head. "Still, think I saw a piece of lent."

"Yes," Danielle answered.

He looked at Danielle, as she was acting stranger than usual. Fiorella nudged her.

"I think black or white," Danielle said. "Those are safe colors."

Danielle pulled her phone out and texted him something. He wrinkled his brow at her as his phone rang. He pulled it and looked at the text, before he crinkled his nose.

"Aw look, he crinkled his nose. Cute!" Fiorella teased.

He walked off and, just to tease them, tossed the shirt out. Fiorella bit her fist and slapped Danielle.

"You're acting like a fan girl." Danielle glared at her.

She got up, picked up the red shirt, and glanced up to catch a glimpse of his well-sculpted upper body.

"I hate you!" She shouted at him.

She heard him laugh, as she balled up the shirt and threw it in the room.

"Pay back," he said.

Portia barked, making Danielle look at the chocolate lab. The dog wagged her tail and walked over her.

"I bet she gets a good peep show," Fiorella mentioned.

"Oh, I'm sure she has deep, dark secrets." Danielle patted Portia.

As Chudamani went on alone first, there was a slight concern that he would collapse on stage and ruin the illusion that he was back a hundred percent. He glanced over at Danielle and gave her a thumb up to let her know he had this.

Danielle held Portia, as the lab eagerly waited for her master to walk off.

"So, you're the translator people are talking about." The delicate voice of Natalia Laterza came from behind.

Danielle glanced over at the soft olive complexion of the Italian singer. She was the trend setter for half the world and often modeled new clothing from her closest friends.

"Yes, I am." Danielle smiled. "Danielle Bennet."

"Natalia Laterza," Natalia said.

She glanced over at Chudamani and smiled. "He's strong you know? He's been through a lot and has conquered it all."

"I have heard…I've seen." Danielle answered.

"I'm glad he has someone there with him. He needs that companionship." Natalia rested her hand on Danielle's shoulder.

Portia barked at Natalia, and the delicate Italian woman knelt to rub her ears.

"And he's very lucky to have this beautiful girl in his life." Natalia smiled as she kissed Portia's nose. "I can never forget how happy he was to receive such a beautiful girl."

Danielle looked at Natalia, as she rubbed Portia's ears.

"I heard that he told you." Natalia looked up at Danielle.

"Yes, he kind of was forced to. He had one in front of me." Danielle frowned and felt the lump return.

"Well, he trusts you now, though timing wasn't the best. He's told people who he thought he could trust, and they ran away."

"His fiancée?"

"Left him at the altar. The note that she wrote was a confession that she could not take care of him. She wasn't meant to take care of someone. He's limited his trust to me, Vicenzo, his brother, and certain people he's worked with."

Danielle nodded and looked at him, as he took a bow. He walked off and Portia ran to him, lightly licking his hand.

"Chudamani?" Danielle gave him a worried look, as he walked briskly.

"Natalia, can you take over?" Antonio came running. "Danielle, come with me…quickly."

She followed his manager, as he followed behind Chudamani. Antonio grabbed a couple of water bottles from a stagehand and handed one to her.

"What's going on?"

"He mentioned he was having problems breathing. He barely finished the song." Antonio pushed open Chudamani's door.

Chudamani sat on the sofa, breathing deeply. He took the ear pieces out of his ear and tossed them to the side. He leaned forward, and Portia sat between his feet. She licked his sweaty face while he continued to inhale large amounts of air.

"Chudamani?" Danielle questioned.

"Drink," Antonio said.

He took the bottle of water and chugged the whole thing without taking a breath. He reached into Portia's vest pocket and pulled out the medication again. Danielle opened the bottle and handed it to him.

"I just needed a moment. My chest was feeling tight, and I couldn't breathe." Chudamani glanced up as Danielle knelt in front of him. "I'm alright, I promise."

She stared at him and grabbed his hands. He looked and seemed to have a shallow breath.

"I'm ok, thank you. I can go back on." Chudamani breathed.

"Are you sure?" Antonio asked.

"Yes, I'm fine." Chudamani slowly stood.

He staggered, but Danielle grabbed his arm. She looked up at him and glanced down at Portia. She seemed calm and still at his feet.

"Portia, is he good?" Danielle asked her.

Portia barked as Danielle smiled. She looked up at him and reached up, cupping his face. Her blue-eyed gaze stared into his hazel one, as she hoped he was telling the truth.

"You have this, Chudamani. I believe in you. Natalia and Vicenzo have your back. Just breathe." She finally broke a smile to encourage him.

He put his hands on hers and nodded.

"I have this." He nodded his head. "I have this."

"Good, now get back on and rock it out!" She patted his cheek.

Chudamani took a deep breath and rolled his shoulders back. "Tell them I'm walking out."

"You got it, boss." Antonio smiled as he let Chudamani walk ahead. "Good job! You got him up again, so let's see if he can keep it."

Danielle shook her head, as Antonio seemed like he was trying to be funny. She whistled for Portia, and they walked to the side of the stage.

CHAPTER SIX

As the days passed and the brisk Italian air began to bare down, Chudamani remained positive that Antonio could get him more appearances to keep up his popularity. The nine shows that he had done scrapped in enough money to prove he was still in the game, so he was back in the studio once more, working on a little bit of a different type of music.

Danielle watched as he sang his heart out. There was so much emotion and expression while he poured his heart out. She could feel hers pound against her chest at the sound.

"Danielle, there's a phone call," Fiorella said. "It's the label."

Danielle nodded and walked to an office. She looked at Fiorella and gave her a nod, shutting the door and lifting the phone to her ear.

"Hello?"

"Danielle, how is our superstar doing?"

"He's doing great! I'm very impressed with how he is mastering the English language. Oh, and he's looking forward to traveling to the States." Danielle avoided the real question.

"That's wonderful, but that's not what I'm asking. By now, you know that the label has had their suspicions about the well-being of Chudamani. We want to know that he is still capable of handling the stress that comes with his fame," the owner of the label asked.

Danielle sat down and glanced out the office, as Chudamani took a break. She breathed deep and looked at the personal items of the studio engineer.

"As a translator, he's perfectly capable of handling whatever language barrier comes his way. And if his mental capability is questioned, then I suggest you do your own test.

But seeing that you are not a doctor, nor a psychologist, then you have to rely on my word.”

There was silence on the other line. Danielle waited to hear what they had to come up with.

“We’ll be in touch, Danielle. Keep up the good work.”

The line went dead, and she let out the breath she had been holding in. She got up and walked out, seeing Chudamani listening to the play back. She leaned against the office door and knew she just signed her termination letter.

“Danielle, come.” Chudamani gestured for her to listen.

She smiled and walked up to him. He closed his eyes as he swayed to the masterpiece in the making. He did air drums and played an imaginary guitar. She laughed a little, and he grabbed her hands, dancing with her.

“It’s good, right?” Chudamani asked.

“I think you have a hit.” Danielle smiled.

“Bravo! We celebrate!” Chudamani twirled her and kissed her cheek.

She blushed and looked at Fiorella, who raised her perfect brow.

“Fiorella, make dinner reservations at Roma’s finest restaurant!” Chudamani turned to her.

“Not your assistant, Chudamani.” Fiorella threw her famous attitude at him.

“Then I guess you don’t want to be in the next video.” He baited her.

“I’d like to see that in writing.” Fiorella smiled and blew a mocking kiss.

She walked off with her phone to her ear. Chudamani looked at Danielle, as her smile faded slightly.

“What is it?” Chudamani asked.

“Your label called. They are thinking you may be a risk with your condition.” Danielle fell to the couch in the studio. "I gave them what I felt was my best report, but I don't feel well about it now."

Chudamani walked over and sat beside her. He put his arm around her, and she leaned her head on his chest.

"We had a good run," Chudamani said. "I can release these songs before they cut me."

Danielle looked at him and shook her head.

"I have a year to change their mind. We've only made it a month; you have a contract. We'll get you into the finest shape we can get." Danielle smiled.

Chudamani lightly pushed back strands of her auburn hair from her face. He smiled and leaned towards her, before placing a kiss on her cheek.

"Everything will be fine." He patted her cheek. "Just watch and see."

He got up and winked at her, going back to singing.

That afternoon, Chudamani took the time to run and clear his mind. He breathed deep as he pushed the negative thoughts away. But the more he thought about everything, the more he pushed himself to go faster and further.

He listened to the drum beats and matched it with his breaths. He felt the struggle to keep going up the steepness of the old city, and his mind shouted at him that he needed to stop. His body ached and, before he knew it, he stumbled.

Chudamani fell and slid across the cobble stone streets. His eyes stared ahead, as he saw two residents rush over. He slowly got up but twisted his ankle.

"I'm fine." He hobbled to a bench.

"Signore Amoretto," Stefano said, rushing over. "Shall I get signora?"

"No, just get some ice, and I could use a hot coffee." Chudamani mentioned.

"You see, you pushed yourself, Chudamani. Stupido! What are you running from?" One of the older residence chastised him.

He smiled and got smart. "I guess I was hoping to run away from you."

She slapped him on the back of the head.

"Stefano, call that American girl who keeps this stupido in check." The older woman snapped.

Chudamani sighed and looked at the tear that he acquired when he slid across the cobble stone street. He dabbed it and winced at the touch.

"Red must be my color, makes all the women go nuts when it's on me." He winked at the older women who came to help him.

Stefano walked out and handed him a hot coffee, and the boy's mother came over and placed ice on Chudamani's ankle.

"You called Danielle?"

"I did. My mother made me, otherwise my grandmother would have smacked me as hard as she smacked you."

"I see we're going to have to work on that." Chudamani looked at the younger man.

It was an hour before Danielle made it into town and saw him being pampered by all the women. She folded her arms and stared at him.

"You look so hurt and weak." Danielle tapped her foot.

"I do not know what it is that makes women flock to me." Chudamani smiled sheepishly.

Stefano walked over and shook his head.

"I have got to learn his tricks. I barely can get the girl in the flower shop to notice me." Stefano folded his arms.

Danielle looked at him and gave the back of his head a smack.

"What was that for?"

"Encouraging him."

Stefano smiled and looked at the women. She shooed them away, and he watched her.

"You're staying home tonight. No celebrating." Danielle threw his arm over her shoulder. "And going on a diet."

"I'll get my father's truck and drive you back, signora." Stefano looked at her eagerly.

"That would be great!"

The young man ran off, and Danielle glanced over Chudamani. She shook her head, seeing the tear with blood stains.

"Tripped. Got so into what I was doing, I wasn't paying attention." Chudamani looked at her. "Shit happens, yes?"

"Apparently it does." Danielle smiled.

Stefano pulled to the front of the café and helped Chudamani into the truck. She climbed into the back and watched as all the women waved to him.

He looked back at Danielle, as she held on to the cab of the truck. He chuckled and looked at the younger man.

"I think she likes you, Chudamani." Stefano looked over at him. "She's pretty, but her style is blinding."

Chudamani slapped him on the back of head. "You never talk about a woman's style."

"You do it all the time. Even their looks—like her butt's too big, her breasts are too small." Stefano laughed.

"Still, don't let them hear you." Chudamani laughed. "It will offend them, apparently."

"So, do you like her?"

Chudamani glanced at Danielle through the review mirror. She sat perfectly in the back of the truck bed, like she had done so before. He had been encouraged by Vicenzo to get out of his slump by sleeping with her. This was for the sake of realizing it didn't have to really mean anything.

"She's a nice girl."

"Is that all?"

"Since when did you decide to grow up?" Chudamani asked.

"Since Danielle came to town. She's really had some effect on everyone. She's strange, but aren't most Americans?"

Chudamani laughed and nodded in agreement.

Stefano pulled up to the apartment complex and helped Danielle out from the back. He then went to help Chudamani out.

"My mother will bring you something for the swelling," Stefano said. "Just put it on with a warm compress."

"What, I can't smoke it?"

"Chudamani," Danielle snapped.

"I was joking."

Chudamani chuckled as he leaned against the iron gate. He stared at Danielle, who seemed half amused by his humor, but there was concern because of his condition. He shrugged it off and pushed away what he was thinking about.

"Thank you, Stefano. I can help him the rest of the way." Danielle smiled as she got him balanced.

Danielle opened the gate and got him through before the daunting task of getting up the stairs. He grabbed the railing and hopped up the steps. She looked after him, waiting for that to end badly.

"You should have taken Portia." Danielle climbed up with him.

"It wasn't a seizure. I just got overly excited and lost track of where my foot went." Chudamani stopped and looked at her. "I'm still a living and breathing person. I'm beginning to feel that you don't see that anymore. Not every incident is because of my condition. Give me credit that I can be stupid without the help of a condition."

"Trust me, I know, but I want you to be careful."

Chudamani climbed up to the third floor, and she pulled the keys out.

"You don't have to keep worrying. I have Portia to do that, plus the other people. It gets exhausting having another person worry about me."

He hobbled to the sofa and put his foot up on the table. He leaned forward and unlaced his shoe to kick it off.

"I'm sorry," Danielle said.

She frowned at him while he pouted like a child. She grabbed some ice and a towel from the lining closet by the laundry room, wrapping it tight before placing it carefully on his twisted ankle.

"Where are all of your bandages and ointments?" Danielle asked.

"Under the sink. Just be warned that other personal items are there," Chudamani mentioned.

"Gross." Danielle rolled her eyes, as he smirked a little.

She walked to the bathroom and dug through the unorganized items. Finding the hydroperoxide and other things she need, she quickly walked over and sat beside him.

"I think you may live," Danielle said. "Sadly, your pants won't."

"Oh, the humanity. Another pair of pants I loved have met an untimely death!" Chudamani dramatically mourned his torn running pants. "What will I do?"

She poured a little hydroperoxide, and he let out a loud shout. She looked at him, leaned forward, and blew on his knee.

"Big baby." She cleaned it, before putting a bandage on the single scratch.

He leaned back and closed his eyes for a moment, and she looked at him with worry, as he seemed to be troubled by something. His eyes said he was fighting something, but she didn't want to pry.

"Do you want to sit here or lay down?" Danielle asked.

"I'm pretty comfortable right here." He opened one eye and looked at her. "What were you doing while I went for a run?"

"Oh, so now you're interested? Funny, because you didn't seem to be earlier." Danielle lightly nudged him. "I was talking to Natalia; we're going to have coffee and shop. Unlike you, she likes my style. It just needs a little tweaking. And I happen to appreciate her style too."

"I hope you two are very happy with each other," Chudamani kidded.

"I don't have a lot of friends here in Italy, so it's nice to be included in things. After all, I get a little crazy spending time with you. I need a day off from you."

"See, I thought it was because you were in love with me."

"You're lucky I don't hit you in your balls again."

He sat up and reached for the ice, staring at the swollen ankle.

"Well, I guess I'll be out of the light for a little." Chudamani smirked at her and gave her leg a pat. "Thanks."

Danielle smiled, reached over, and kissed his cheek.

"You need to shave."

She lightly brushed his cheek with her hand and stared at the pepper color in his more-than-a-five-o'clock shadow. He gazed at her, as she brushed her hand through the stubble. He reached up and grabbed her hand, kissing the palm of it.

Danielle reached over and pressed her lips against his. He pushed forward and deepened the kiss.

It was the hard knock that pulled them back to reality. She quickly got up and rushed to the door to answer, expecting it to be Stefano with the herbs.

She opened the door, though, it was not the young man, but a polished, uniformed, baby-faced man. Her eyes lit up at the blue-eyed, uniformed man, and she wrapped her arms tightly around him.

"Ty!" She squealed with excitement. "What are you doing here?"

"I came to see my baby-sister." He wrapped his arms around her.

"Come in," she said, shuffling him in.

He smiled and walked into the apartment. His eyes scanned the small living area, and then made eye-contact with Chudamani.

"Chudamani, this is my big brother, Tyler," She said. "Ty, this is Chudamani Amoretto, my client."

"Pleasure to meet you. Looks like you've taken a stumble; is that old age or an accident?"

"Cobble stone tends to be objective when you pound your feet on it." Chudamani raised his gaze to him. "Pleasure to meet you, but it looks like it may be time for my nap…being old and all."

He started to get up, and Danielle rushed over to help him get a steady footing. He looked at her and gestured that he had it. He stared down at her with a softened gaze. Her gaze seemed distant due to the visitor and filled with concern

"Go visit with your brother; I'll be fine. I have Portia." Chudamani pushed back a fallen lock of her auburn hair.

"Are you sure?"

"I could take the time to rest up. We'll be busy for the next month or so. I have a video to film and a couple of big shows with Vicenzo. You need a life outside of watching me." Chudamani ignored what happened.

"Ok, I'll check on you later." Danielle looked into his eyes and was just about to pat his cheek, but she dropped her hand.

He gave a nod and limped towards his bed room. He watched as she walked back to the living room. His brow wrinkled, and he felt this unwanted feeling gnawing at him—the whole reason he had fallen.

"He's your boss?" He heard Tyler say.

"Yes, he's my boss."

Chudamani shut the door once he got into his room. Leaning against the door, he closed his eyes tightly and placed his hand on his chest. He heard Portia groan and jump off the bed to lick his other hand.

"I'm fine, Portia. Go lay down." He rubbed her ears. "Let's take a nap."

She wagged her tail and jumped back into the unmade bed. He sat down on it and rubbed the stubble of hair that slowly was coming back from his treatment. Chudamani fell back into his bed, his gaze staring up at the white ceiling. His breaths steadied, and Portia leaned her head on his chest. He put one arm around her and fell into a light sleep, listening to the voices of brother and sister talking outside of the room.

Danielle looked at her brother while she set a cup of tea in front of him. He looked back at her, as she stirred the honey into her white cup.

"Why are you still here, Dani?" Tyler asked. "Why aren't you home?"

" 'Cause there's nothing left there." Danielle looked at him. "You are not home, and Mama doesn't talk to me after what happened. I don't want to go back to an empty house, Ty."

"Move in with me. You don't have to go back to that home." Tyler reached for her hand and grabbed it. "Plus, it beats being nurse maid to someone like that guy. He's an unknown in the equation."

Danielle lifted the white cup to her lips and shook her head. She stared at the ribbons on her brother's uniform and smiled. He was climbing the ranks and working on his next career.

"Why are you here, Ty?"

"'Cause I needed to see my little sister. I'm on leave until tomorrow and thought I'd drop by. I followed the paper trail to this small apartment. I mean, where do you sleep?"

"It's a two-bedroom apartment. He lives a simple life when he comes home."

Tyler looked at her and wrinkled his brow at her. He was fifteen years older than her and knew his sister ran from things. He had lost his good friend too, and she forgot that.

"He's not going to help you find peace, Dani. He's a messed up old man who is washed up in the industry. If you try to think, for a moment, that peace is secured here in Rome, then you're are just as crazy as he is."

"How dare you!" Danielle snapped. "I came here to do a job, and I have a client that needs my help. For your information, you don't have any right to tell me what to do. You don't know what hell I have gone through. Harrison's mother blames me for his death, and his father said I was just a white-trash bitch that married him to take his money."

"He was my friend too, Dani. Don't tell me that you are the only one suffering." Tyler glared at her with his intense blue-eyed gaze.

Danielle breathed deep, as her brother's temper surfaced. She looked away from his judgement.

"Dani, please come home and do your duties. Mama needs you now, and she's changed since you've last seen her. She just wants what was best for you. Dad left a huge hole in her, and I can't take care of her anymore. She needs a daughter, not a son."

"I'm not Mama's keeper. I have a life here in Rome. I am staying here with Chudamani and fulfilling my contract with the label."

Tyler shifted uncomfortably at the mention of the fifty-something-year-old, Italian. Danielle watched as he looked around.

"He's going to hurt you, and you will never be the same. I hope I don't have to come clean up the pieces. I just want you to stop running from whatever it is you are running from." Tyler rubbed his eyes.

Danielle stood up and walked towards the door. She looked away from her older brother and waited for him to take the hint.

"I'm not giving up on you, Dani," Tyler said. "You're my baby sister, and I take care of my family. What's he going to do when you're not his employee?"

"I guess I won't know until my contract is over." Danielle looked at him. "Please leave. I have to get ready for dinner."

Tyler nodded and walked to the door. He reached over and kissed her cheek, before walking out. Danielle shut the door hard and picked up the mugs of unfinished tea. She sighed and looked at the mugs in the sink, feeling judgement from family. Her hands gripped the edge of the counter to vent her anger.

She stormed off to her room with fire in her eyes. Her mind ran wild, as she couldn't shake what her brother said. He wanted to make sure she was alright, but he also wanted her to come home and take care of their mother, because he couldn't deal with her. He was their father's son—always taking up the ranks to keep the women in check. Old fashioned and demanding.

Then there were the emotions that continued to seep into her thoughts. The kiss that she and Chudamani shared. There were feelings there that she had not felt in years. Her eyes became scared as she looked at herself in the mirror. Who was the woman before her? She looked like her, but there was something different about this woman. There were more questions than answers, as her hand touched her lips. She had to ignore these feelings and keep working with a clear mind.

After an hour of not able to focus on reading again, she went to check on Chudamani. She still felt responsible for his wellbeing. Danielle walked quietly down to his room and opened the creaky door. She peeked in to see Portia laying with her head on his side. She listened to the steady breathing and turned to close the door.

"Danielle," she heard him mumble her name.

She turned and opened the door to see him open his eyes. "Yes?"

"Don't take this the wrong way, but your brother is a tool." He shifted a little.

"He's a solider. They know how to follow orders, and that's what he's doing." Danielle folded her arms. "Always has been a solider."

"My brother didn't turn out that way, and he was in the Italian army."

"He's also a priest, so I hardly count that."

She looked at Portia, as the lab thumped her tail on the bed. She stared at Danielle with her helpless look in her eyes.

"Is your ankle alright?" She asked.

"I twisted it; I didn't break it."

Portia finally muffed at Danielle, and she walked over to pet her. Chudamani looked at Danielle and scooted over. Portia moved to the end of the bed and muffed. He patted the bed and Danielle stared at him.

"Lay down. You look like you went through the ringer and back." He looked at her. "I already told you, I don't bite."

Danielle sat, and he looked at her.

"No, lay down."

She sighed and laid on her side, and Chudamani slipped his arms around her. She stared at the wall, still feeling awkward laying in his bed. She knew Fiorella would have a field day with what was happening.

Chudamani laid his head just beside hers. She could feel the warmth of his breath on the back of her neck.

"Relax, Danielle. I'm not going to put the moves on you," Chudamani muttered. "Just rest your eyes."

Danielle closed her eyes and listened to the silence that surrounded them. She finally relaxed and let her mind settle on nothing. It was the first moment that she felt completely comfortable around him and not alert. The tides had changed; she was completely letting her guard down and trusting someone she had barely known.

CHAPTER SEVEN

The next morning slipped in between the space where the blackout curtains met. It lightly traced their faces and warmed their skin.

Chudamani opened his eyes, feeling the warmth of a second body in bed with him. He looked over and saw Portia sleeping on his feet, but also the sleeping woman beside him. He gave a weak smile as he pulled her close to him. It was his first reaction too slowly wake her up, but he did not want to disturb her. He was completely alright holding the petite woman in his arms.

It had been six months since he even held a woman in his arms. Most the women that he was seen with scurried away before they even made it to his bed, and it made him feel as though he was not worth going past the living area. So, Chudamani built a wall between himself and those who wanted to be with him to live a simple life.

He lightly stroked her head and took the moment to just hold a woman without trying to push the boundaries. He did not want to give her a chance to second guess what happened.

Danielle opened her eyes and moaned a little. She felt a hold around her waist and the warm breaths on the back of her neck. Her eyes became wide, as she looked to see his arms around her and realized *she* was in *his* room.

"Chudamani," she whispered.

He slightly moaned a little as he shifted.

"Did we...?" Danielle's voice trailed off with question.

"You're still dressed, aren't you?" He mumbled.

Danielle looked at her clothes still on. She looked over at him, as he opened his eyes.

"Then, no, we didn't sleep together."

She shifted and turned to face him, nearly touching his nose.

"You talk in your sleep," Chudamani mentioned. "It's a little distracting."

Danielle smiled, reached up, and stroked the scruff on his face.

"I'm sorry," she whispered.

"For what?" Chudamani asked.

"For everything you have been through." Danielle's eyes became slightly sadden.

Chudamani reached up and pushed back some locks behind her ear. He smiled and kissed her nose.

"I don't live in the past anymore, especially when the sun is shining," Chudamani stated.

His eyes were filled with wonder, and the sun caught the glimmer of hope that most people get when they have an epiphany. She felt a smile pull at her lips, as he spoke words of comfort.

Portia groaned and Chudamani reached over and patted her stomach. He sat up and Portia jumped up to wedge herself between Danielle and Chudamani. The six-year-old lab rolled on her back and wiggled. Danielle reached over and rubbed her stomach.

"Come, Portia, let's eat breakfast." Chudamani whistled.

Portia jumped over Danielle and sat at the door. He got out of bed and opened the door to let her out. He looked at Danielle and raised his brow.

"Aren't you hungry?" He asked.

Danielle nodded and got out of bed. She walked behind Chudamani, who walked with a slight limp.

"You look like you are walking fine," Danielle mentioned.

There was a loud knock on the door, and Portia barked loudly. Chudamani walked over and opened the door to see a not-so-pleased Italian woman.

"I'm sorry, did I miss the memo that we weren't going to do fine-dining yesterday?" Fiorella walked past him.

"Come in, if you please." Chudamani muttered sarcastically at the unhappy woman.

"Fiorella, I meant to call." Danielle glanced up at her friend, as she realized she had forgotten to fill her in.

"So, what happened you two decided to stay in and let me be the fool?" Fiorella looked at both as she vented.

Chudamani walked to the kitchen and made Portia breakfast, before he started on something for himself and Danielle.

"Breakfast, Fiorella?" Chudamani.

"No, I have a dress to fit into for an event. The label has also been trying to call you, Danielle. They want you to stay on with Chudamani for another six months after the contract is over."

Fiorella pulled out a thick packet of paper.

"And they've offered you a reasonable deal, if you ask me." Fiorella placed it on the table. "Your manager will be looking it over. I'd take it, especially in your condition, Chudamani."

He stopped making breakfast and looked at Fiorella. He walked over to see the stapled letter paper clipped to the first ten pages. He swallowed the lump that climbed up.

"What condition?" Chudamani asked.

"Oh, come now, don't think you can play that game. You have a dog that follows you; even I am not blind." Fiorella rolled her eyes in his direction.

Chudamani shook his head and turned the stove off. He cursed under his breath and tossed the breakfast into the trash.

"Chudamani?" Danielle questioned.

"Who told them?" He continued to play like they did not know.

"Stop the games, Chudamani." Fiorella folded her thin arms.

"I never brought Portia to a meeting with my label." Chudamani pointed to Portia. "So, someone told them."

Fiorella shrugged, and Danielle looked at him nervously, as he seemed furious. She walked towards him and lifted the contract. Her eyes skimmed through the exposed letter with the head of the label's signature. He looked at Danielle while she read the notice.

"Full disclosure of your condition." Danielle mentioned.

"My condition doesn't affect my music."

"But it does your contract with them." Fiorella shifted her weight. "Just look it over and talk about it with your manager. But you aren't getting a better deal."

Chudamani shook his head and lit the stove as he held the contract over the flame. Fiorella rolled her eyes and muttered to herself.

"Don't be so dramatic, Chudamani," Fiorella sighed. "It would be discovered sooner or later. Plus, they probably already had someone tell them. They just wanted to see if you'd come clean. But good on you for keeping this a big secret. I now have a mess to clean up because of you, so take the deal."

He tossed it on the table and looked at Danielle.

"I need to take Portia out," he mentioned. "Don't worry, I won't have an episode for you to take to your boss."

He whistled and hooked Portia up with her vest. He slammed the door, walking out into the brisk cold.

"He really lives up to his reputation," Fiorella mentioned.

"Chudamani's just upset. His trust level is very low."

"When did you find out?"

"He had an episode in front of me. I don't know what set it off. He told me about it, and I accepted him for who he is. He's not a broken man like everyone says he is."

Fiorella nodded and looked at the seared edges of the contract. She sat down and looked at Danielle.

"Weren't you wearing that yesterday?" Fiorella asked.

Danielle wrinkled her brow, slightly confused about her friend's question.

"No, something similar," Danielle denied.

Fiorella smiled as a string of laughter escaped her painted lips. She stood up and wrapped her arms around her friend.

"You slept with him?" Fiorella questioned. "Please, tell me you did. Was he what the rumors say, that he's really good?"

"Fiorella, I did not sleep with him. I fell asleep on the couch this morning and hadn't changed." Danielle folded her arms.

Fiorella leaned forward and took a whiff.

"Smells like his cologne," Fiorella commented. "A very manly cologne, none the less. You can't deny that."

Danielle rolled her eyes and pushed her friend away. She lit the stove and pulled out the eggs, the already prepared batter that he made the night before.

"Look, see if you can convince him to take the deal. It really is a good deal."

"Signing that contract would mean defeat and that he is a broken product. Fiorella, he's healthy."

"They don't think so, Danielle." Fiorella folded her arms. "They see him as a product with an expiration date. All artists have an expiration date…I've seen it. Eventually, they'll just be washed up, singing at cafes and remembering the 'good old days'."

Danielle shrugged and hugged her friend.

"He's not one of them. He's got several years until that time comes."

"I hope so." Fiorella smiled, and she gave Danielle's cheek a pat.

"If you didn't sleep with him, what happened?"

Danielle shook her head and pointed to the door. Fiorella shrugged and picked up her purse. She walked out just as Chudamani was walking in.

"Oh, Pietra asked about you. She said she'll be ready for the video at eight tomorrow." Fiorella's look of disgust just confirmed on how much she hated Pietra.

"Great. She'll be the only one there, because we're shooting it at night." Chudamani smiled. "I changed the time because I wanted something different."

"Great! I love to see that stuck up bitch get the wrong information." Fiorella smiled, full of amusement.

Chudamani unhooked Portia and took a seat, as Danielle finished up breakfast. She leaned forward and fed Portia a little bacon before making a plate for Chudamani.

"Are we going to talk about what happened yesterday?" He questioned.

Danielle looked over her shoulder.

"What happened? You fell."

She looked away, knowing where he was going with the conversation. She was not ready to go over that topic just yet. In fact, she wanted it to just die on the vine. It was a moment of weakness; there was nothing but friendship.

"What happened before your brother's surprised appearance." Chudamani pried more.

Danielle remained ignorant about the topic at hand. She fixed a plate for herself, before pouring two cups of coffee. She set the hot cups on the table and grabbed her plate.

"Don't forget, I'm going shopping with Natalia. You need a day off from me as well. Why don't you go visit your brother?" Danielle lifted a piece of bacon.

"He's busy preaching to the lost and sad. I'll give Vicenzo a call and see what he's doing." Chudamani answered.

She smiled and looked down at her plate, avoiding his gaze.

###

In the late morning, Danielle and Chudamani went their separate ways once they got to Rome.

"Dinner?" Chudamani asked.

Danielle looked at him, and he stood more confident for that moment. He lightly brushed his hand over the stubble of hair on his head. She walked towards him and looked up to meet his hazel-eyed gaze.

"Yes," she said. "What are you cooking?"

"Anything you'd like." Chudamani folded his arms. "I'd like to try your type of food sometime, but I'm cooking."

Danielle smiled, as he seemed to try his hand at something she may like.

"Surprise me." Danielle tucked her arms behind her back. "I like surprises."

"You like playing games." He leaned back on his good ankle.

"So, do you."

"Danielle!" Natalia's voice came from across the station.

Danielle and Chudamani looked over as Natalia came in their direction. She smiled and kissed Chudamani's cheek, before giving his arm a slight brush.

"No, Portia?" She asked.

"Not today, I'll be fine." Chudamani smiled weakly.

Danielle looked at Natalia, as she slightly hid her concern for him. He gave her a kiss on the cheek and made some excuse to get out of the discomfort of the situation.

"I'll be fine." Chudamani waved. "Have fun!"

Danielle frowned as she looked at the forty-three-year-old singer. She shook her head and turned to Danielle with a new look of hope.

"So, I thought we could meet my stylist first and see what style you'd like to add to your wardrobe," Natalie said.

"Great! Lead the way." Danielle's voice was filled with excitement.

The two women walked off, and Chudamani watched from the distance before going the opposite direction. He found the bustling city brought life to his cluttered mind. He walked across the busy streets to a Roman café just around the corner of his favorite music shop. He wanted to make his own strides and felt alive more than ever.

"Buongiorno, Chudamani," a waitress greeted him. "It has been awhile since you've been seen sitting in this spot."

"Buongiorno, Nicola. Yes, it has been awhile. I've kept myself busy with life." Chudamani looked at the young waitress. "How is your sister?"

"She's doing well. She and her husband are traveling. And you have a new woman in your life?"

"Afraid that was another life time that I could have that hope." Chudamani frowned and pulled his coat tighter.

"Are you well?"

"As well as I could be. I'm standing on my own two feet and trying to adapt to the lifestyle these new singers keep." He smiled as he lied about the episode he had.

Nicola smiled and pulled a chair out to sit beside him. She wrinkled her brow and reached over to pat his cheek.

"I am deeply sorry for what happened. It must have been a shock to stand in front of family and friends, just to have someone tell you she would not be coming." Nicola's softened green colored eyes were an exact match as her twin sister's. "I read the note and found it harsh."

"And it is over with. I am moving on." Chudamani wrinkled his brow. "She is free and doesn't have to take care of me. I have people to do that if I need it. It takes a village to raise me."

Nicola smiled and gave a nod of her head. She stood and gave his shoulder a pat, before running to get orders for others, plus his.

The sudden chimes of distant church bells rang out, calling to the lost and lonely. He looked in the distant and admired the sound. His desire, though, was not to run like a whipped dog wanting to be cradled by its master. He had vowed that this was not right moment to return; he needed more time.

Yet, they chimed again for the noon hour, and the songs they sang were of heaven sent. He often recorded the bells for background sounds in his recording. The church choir made an appearance on several occasions during live recordings.

"Well, look who is without his companion," Vicenzo's voice came from off the streets.

Chudamani looked over and extended his hand to his friend.

"Where is the charming girl?" Vicenzo asked.

Chudamani looked at him. "Portia or Danielle?"

"Well, both."

Vicenzo pulled a chair out and took a seat. Chudamani noticed that Vicenzo had finally bent to his wife's wishes and got rid of the fur he called a goatee.

"I see the baby-face has returned." Chudamani gestured to signify that he shaved.

"Yes, Angelica has finally given me a choice—the scruff or she would refuse our twice-a-week love making. And I refused to be denied that." Vicenzo patted his own cheek. "So, here I am, smooth as a bambino's bottom. And I do miss the youthful face, but I also wish to have a little."

Chudamani chuckled as his friend frowned at not having just a little scruff.

"It is nearing the harsh winter; why not keep it?"

"Perhaps it is a little too rough." Vicenzo smiled big.

"Youth is what she wants to see. Maybe you will move your ass faster to the right spot on stage. It was holding you back." Chudamani chuckled with great amusement. "I have already been told it was time for a shave."

"Please, you tell whoever told you so that you are your own man." Vicenzo hit the table and folded his arms.

"Yes, well, I do tend to listen to whoever is talking."

Nicola walked over and put down the hot coffee. Vicenzo looked up at her and slightly jumped.

"Very funny, Vicenzo!" She slapped him with the tray on the back. "I'm sure your mother had the same look when she saw your face."

"I do miss these chats, Nicola. Did you spit in his drink?" Vicenzo asked. "'Cause your sister would have if she saw him."

"Vaffanculo!" Nicola cursed.

"That position has already been filled, Nicola. I see my wife being very happy when she does so." Vicenzo smiled. "And unlike your sister, my wife didn't leave me at the altar for shitty reasons."

"Nice," Chudamani muttered.

Nicola slapped Vicenzo across the face and did spit on him.

"We're all pretty here!" Chudamani handed Vicenzo a napkin.

"I think my dear friend has made a better choice than your slutty sister, who will jump if her husband says so."

Nicola looked at Vicenzo, as he raised his brow at her. She turned to look at Chudamani, who seemed shocked.

"You didn't hear about the new girl? Well, then I guess I'll keep talking about her." Vicenzo smiled.

Chudamani kicked Vicenzo in the shin, and he looked over to wink at him.

"She's a translator, molta bella! If I were not a married man, I'd certain try to win this dame's heart. He's written her a sweet ballad…guess he never did that for your sister." Vicenzo folded his arms. "Best sex of his life too."

"Vicenzo!" Chudamani growled.

"Yeah, stuff your sister wouldn't do for him, she'll do."

"You are a pig, Vicenzo!" Nicola snapped.

She walked off, and Chudamani gave him a wide-eyed glance. Vicenzo chuckled a little before slipping on his sunglasses.

"Now, you must bring her everywhere. She's going to play the part very well—meek and humble, but a tigress in the night hours." Vicenzo smirked.

"You are a fucking moron, Vicenzo, a fucking moron."

"Where is she?"

"She's with Natalia; they went shopping."

"You let Natalia take your woman out for a shopping trip? Danielle will come back a changed woman once she's done with her. You're in big trouble, Chudamani, big trouble. Girls talk, and, when they talk, men quiver at the very thought. They'll dissect you and try to fix you."

Chudamani shook his head with amusement; his friend had been married twice. His current wife was a saint for dealing with his crazy idea of what women did.

"Look, I'm just saying, Natalia will change her into that woman you've been resisting for how long? You can't fight that feeling, Chudamani. Got to get back in the game."

"I'm not sure I'm ready, and there's a possibility…"

"It's Chudamani, right?" A familiar voice was heard not too far.

Chudamani glanced over to see the one man that was fighting to bring Danielle back to the States. His pressed uniform made the women go weak in the knees, and his eyes were like ice to those who came near his little sister.

"Cazzo!" Chudamani muttered.

"What?" Vicenzo looked over his shoulder to see the younger man. "Chi è?"

"Grande Fratello," he mentioned.

"Cazzo."

Tyler walked over and extended his hand to Chudamani, who reached out to shake his hand.

"Buongiorno, Tyler," Chudamani greeted him.

Tyler looked over at Vicenzo, as the other man sized him up. He looked back at Chudamani.

"Is he alright?"

"He gets a little nervous around new people; we're working with him." Chudamani looked at Vicenzo, wrinkling his brow at him.

"Special, huh? We had a cousin like that once—took too many blows to the head." Tyler looked at Vicenzo pointedly.

"He's had too many as a singer. This is Vicenzo Scordato, my good friend. He's family." Chudamani introduced Vicenzo.

"Ah, family, like the God Father, right? All you people are like family." Tyler looked at him. "Tyler Guillot, U.S. Airforce."

Vicenzo stood up and extended his hand to Tyler.

"You Yanks think we're all the same," Vicenzo said, "but we aren't. We aren't like this 'God Father' you talk about. In fact, some of us actually understand when we are being insulted. So, spare me that ignorant introduction, Staff Sargent."

Tyler blinked at Vicenzo, looking over his sunglasses.

"Pilot for three years, flew several missions before you were even a gleam in your mother's eyes, baby blues." Vicenzo pushed off his jacket and rolled up his left sleeve.

"Got shot in the arm too when a mission went rye. Natives were restless and shot me. So, cowboy, don't go showing off your ribbons until you've crawled through a sweaty jungle to get intel."

"Put the measuring stick away, Vicenzo," Chudamani said.

"Well, look at you, sharpshooter. Didn't see you as a solider boy." Tyler extended his hand to Vicenzo.

"Shake," Chudamani muttered.

Vicenzo wrinkled his nose and extended his hand to Tyler. He pulled his hand back.

"So, I'm looking for Danielle." Tyler turned to Chudamani. "Where is she?"

"She's with a friend of mine, Natalia Laterza. They are having a girls' day. Needed a break from each other." Chudamani leaned back into the iron back chair. "You know, she likes it here; she's comfortable here."

Tyler looked at Chudamani, as he seemed comfortable, too, with her there. He reached into his back pocket and pulled his phone out.

"Look, I appreciate you standing up for her, but she belongs at home. She's got family responsibilities. And we don't very much care for Danielle roaming the streets of a foreign city without guidance. She's had her fun time being a free woman, but her family needs her. And for one, she needs to get her head on straight and get her duties done."

Chudamani looked at Vicenzo and back at Tyler. He stood up and Vicenzo joined in standing.

"Cowboy, go back to the ranch and try pulling that John Wayne crap somewhere else. It doesn't fly here in Rome." Vicenzo looked at him.

"Are you threatening me?" Tyler asked.

"Maybe." Vicenzo raised his brow.

"And I don't live on a ranch, you fucker. I'm from the fucking south."

"Can I hit him now, Chudamani?"

"No."

"I swear to the big guy upstairs, I'm going to beat him."

"Vicenzo, he's not worth it. Danielle is not going home; she's under contract with the label. She couldn't, if she tried to, get out of it. It's a fifteen-thousand-Euro contract that, if she breaks, will lose her a lot of money. And with what she does for a living, I see her being pretty content."

Chudamani zipped up his coat and gave Vicenzo a pat on the shoulder.

"Have a good day, Tyler." Chudamani gave him a back-hand wave.

Vicenzo gave him the highly offensive under the chin flip off. He walked off and caught up with Chudamani.

"You realize he thinks you slept with his sister, right?"

"Yup, but I haven't yet, so I'm pretty safe."

"You could never satisfy my sister like her husband did!" Tyler shouted. "You've gone limp old man!"

Chudamani felt his fists ball up, and he bit hard not to go back and show Tyler just how old he was. Vicenzo grabbed his shoulder and shook his head.

"Not worth it," Vicenzo said. "The limp noodle is just trying to get to you."

He took a deep breath and walked on.

Danielle and Natalia sat at a restaurant that overlooked the perfect scene of Rome.

"Thank you so much, Natalia!" Danielle gratefully expressed her appreciation.

"I think you will find these styles are perfect for your colorful side and the Italian lifestyle we have here in Rome.

Not to mention, you were not exactly wearing the right undergarments for someone of your age." Natalia smiled.

Danielle shook her head and looked away.

"Danielle, you are doing a lot for Chudamani. He is happy, and life can only get better for him. He is more willing to risk his career than he had in the past, so healthy looking, but there is still much he needs to improve on. But, I believe you have seen his sunny disposition." Natalia reached for her glass of wine.

Danielle nodded and sighed. She was distant about the unexpected kiss she shared with Chudamani. She had broken the vow of being in mourning for her husband.

"What is it?" Natalia reached over and grabbed her hand.

"I kissed him," she confessed. "It was a moment of weakness."

"Oh, that is not a bad thing; it is attraction." Natalia smiled. "You are young, and he's mature. It is natural to be attracted to someone of his age. It isn't like you are married and slept with him. It was a kiss."

"You don't understand; I am widowed. My husband was killed while he was on assignment. I also lost a child two months later, and I really haven't been the same. I can't trust myself." Danielle felt her throat swell with a lump.

Natalia's gaze became soft, and she gave Danielle's hand a squeeze.

"When did this happen?"

"Three years ago. It was sudden that I took a job here in Italy. When I was assigned to be Chudamani's translator, I could only be angry again."

"Why?"

"Because my husband and I were going to take a trip to Italy. He mentioned he was willing to go see a concert. One of my favorite singers."

"Chudamani,"

"Yes, I was horrible to him. I thought I was being mocked."

"Maybe you weren't being mocked. Maybe he pointed you here to help someone else who needed it. Call it a sign that maybe it was time for you to give someone a chance to find happiness and, in return, find your own happiness." Natalia smiled. "You have heard the saying 'God works in mysterious ways'. So, why not embraced that? It's fitting that Chudamani's brother is a man of the cloth. Go see him and tell him…He could give you guidance."

Danielle still felt guilty; the idea that maybe it was time to give someone else a chance only presented itself once before her.

"Trust what you believe, but don't let it keep you from what may happen." Natalia smiled.

The charm of the ancient city had made an imprint on Danielle's heart. It had become her home and salvation. The reminder of a once and great empire remained in several still-standing structures that were tucked away under newer ones.

"Danielle, tell Chudamani how you feel," Natalia said. "He needs to know. You deserve to see if he feels the same way. And if I know Chudamani like I do, I've already seen how much he trusts you."

Danielle nodded, and Natalia reached over and kissed her cheek.

"You'll see, things will become clear."

The church bells of Santa Anna's rang throughout the piazza. Natalia pointed to the doors that were letting out for mass.

"I believe your answers may be found there. Sunday mass is out, and you are available for a chat with the good father." Natalia smiled with a wink. "Go. I'll catch up with you at Chudamani's studio session. We're doing a duet along with Vicenzo."

Danielle slightly shook her head.

"What?"

"I think Vicenzo may be egging Chudamani on."

"He's a crazy bastard, but he's looking out for his friend. Vicenzo was the first to visit Chudamani in the hospital after his first round of treatment. They are like brothers separated at birth. Don't let him get to you."

Danielle nodded, and Natalia went on her way. She looked over and saw Francis sending off his flock of followers. She walked towards the young brother, and he looked over at her approaching form.

"Danielle, how good to see you!" He greeted her. "I see Chudamani and Portia are not with you."

"Took a day to get some fresh air. Natalia and I went shopping."

"Natalia is such a wonderful person to be friends with. Very insightful." Francis smiled and welcomed her into the church. "I get the sense you have something to ask."

She gave a smile and nodded. He walked her the very last pew in the church and invited her to sit. He pulled down the kneeler and made the sign of the cross. She did the same and closed her eyes.

"Dear Heavenly Father, bless this woman that she may find her way down the path you have chosen for her. Let her show you what is in her heart and that you will help her see it is what she truly wants. I ask this in your name, Amen." Francis prayed.

He once more made the sign of the cross and kissed the rosery he held in his hand. She smiled and came to sit down.

"What is it that you want to ask?" Francis asked as he sat.

Danielle's saddened eyes stared at the younger brother. She felt her heart swell with pain as she tried to stay loyal to her dead husband.

"I feel guilty," she stated.

"Why?"

"I lost my husband three years ago and a child. I promised my husband he'd be the only one I would ever love. I wanted to just stay away from the life I had, so I ran here for a job, a place where my husband and I were planning to go for a second honeymoon. And it seems I am more comfortable here than I am in my own country. I've fallen in love with Rome and Italy, and I've only been fighting what I've promised." Danielle looked at him timidly. "Worst is, I believe I have feelings for a man that reminds me of my promise."

Francis watched her struggle with what she thought was supposed to protect her. He reached over and placed his hand on her shoulder.

"My brother has that effect on people," Francis said. "It's his superpower."

Danielle stared at him, and he just smiled in return.

"Danielle, there was a time when my brother was the one who believed his life was destined to be in misery. We all go through this in our lives, but it's the life we stumble on. I do not know your husband, but I do not believe he would want you to suffer like you are. I believe he would want you to live a life that would to make you happy."

Francis looked forward and stared at the altar before him. The beauty of the old altar was inherited from the former priest. He admired everything about it, from the wooden tabernacle to the beautiful statues that surrounded the church.

"Did your husband agree to making such a promise after his death?" Francis asked as he looked to her.

"No," Danielle answered. "It was on my own."

"A promise is received by two."

"What do you mean?"

"My vows as priest were to God, All Mighty and myself. Though you could not hear Him talking to me directly, I heard Him accept my vows and duties. Your husband's soul had already departed from this world. He did not have a chance to accept your promise. I believe in a second chance and that perhaps your prayers of sadness are being answered, telling you it is alright to move on." Francis looked at her. "You are a brave woman, Danielle, death is hard to overcome, but we weather the storm and go on. Do you love your husband?"

"Yes, of course!"

"You can love your deceased husband by keeping his memory alive in your heart, but live the life you want."

Danielle breathed deep as she swallowed back the tears.

"Live, Danielle, live a full life and find what God has planned for you. Look for signs in everyday life."

Danielle nodded, and Francis gave her cheek a pat.

"He's very fond of you, Danielle. Our chats often end with how much you have made his life improve."

The church doors opened, and Francis looked over to see Chudamani standing there.

"Go with God, Danielle. I shall pray for His help to guide you." Francis made the sign of the cross in front of him.

"Thank you, Padre."

Danielle turned and looked to see Chudamani standing there. He walked towards her, and she lifted her gaze to meet his.

"Chudamani, you are late, but come and walk with me!" Francis greeted him.

Danielle smiled. "I'll go and take Portia out, and then we can cook dinner together."

"I would like that." Chudamani kept his gaze on her.

"Then I'll see you at the apartment." Danielle smiled.

He reached into his back pocket and pulled the silver key. She reached up and he placed the key in her hand, lightly dragging his hand over hers.

Danielle smiled and walked out the church doors, while Chudamani watched her disappear into the crowd.

"Come," Francis said. "I think it is time we had a chat about Danielle."

Chudamani looked over at his brother, who stood there waiting for him.

CHAPTER EIGHT

As the Italian winter began to file in, the briskness of the cool air the swept from the north brought cooler temperatures to the southern part of the country. Chudamani had begun a regional tour to break out of routine and to release his newest single from the upcoming album. He refused to sign the contract, even though it was advised by his manager who knew everything about what was going on.

"Again!" Chudamani, overly spirited, told his band. "I'm not hearing the excitement!"

"Chudamani, we're tired," his guitar player remarked. "If you keep running this again and again, we'll do the exact same thing."

"Then change it so we can move along," Chudamani said. "The audience needs to feel it."

He looked over at Antonio, who shook his head. He could see the disappointment in the seventy-something's face. Of course, most of the disappointment was not from his reworking the set, but the continuation of refusing to sign the contract.

"Chudamani, it is perfect." Antonio walked towards the stage. "The audience will love this version of the song."

"It isn't perfect," Chudamani stated. "I can hear it differently."

"Take five everyone; I need to speak to him," Antonio said.

They all sighed with relief while the older man walked toward him. Chudamani was tired too, but his spirited nature refused to give up. He wanted his grand comeback to be remembered after he was dethroned by the new music of younger singers.

"If you keep pushing yourself, Chudamani, you'll have another episode. You can't handle a break down on stage."

Chudamani sat on the edge of the stage as he wiped the sweat off is face. The older man looked at him and gave Chudamani's cheek a pat.

"God rest your father's soul, Chudamani, but he raised a stubborn asshole. He would not want his son to go down in flames. And I believe you need to sit to think about your future. If you give the label what they want, you can freely do as you please with it." Antonio looked at the hazel-eyed singer.

"If I sign that contract, they win. I have to report my condition as the start of the end of my career."

"Let Danielle work with them. She has pull, and that friend of hers, Fiorella, has some too. She's been scouting, and now she's been promoted to assistant promoter. Give her fire to work with and ignore what they think is broken." Antonio looked at him. "Have you slept any?"

Chudamani looked away and shook his head.

"Not since Danielle has gone for a week to visit her family in the States," Chudamani said.

"Then I suggest you bring Portia wherever you go," Antonio advised.

Chudamani brushed his hands through the more-than-stubble on his head. The five o'clock shadow that he had was now rough-looking stubble. His routine had changed once more when Danielle took a week off to attend to family matters in her home country.

"Go take a break and get some fresh air. Pounding your musicians for a perfect sound won't help," Antonio said. "Go visit your mother; she's been asking about her Chudamani."

"You would know; you live with the old bat."

"That's not very fair, Chudamani. She only worries about you and what you did with your life. You had a full-ride to that English University everyone goes crazy about."

"To play football, but I wanted music," Chudamani sighed.

"She wanted you to have the best, so don't get attitude with me, you bastard."

Chudamani chuckled and raised his brow at his manager, who was true family on his father's side. The old bastard married his mother six years after his father passed. He was a college explorer until he threw in the towel to play music. His brother thrilled that his mother was no longer living in sin and finally married again.

"Get out of here, kid," Antonio said, "or I'll box your ears like your father did."

Chudamani jumped off the stage and walked through the floor seating. He glanced over at his manager and shook his head.

As he got out, the harsh wind slapped him in the face. He stepped back and took in the cold air, releasing a harsh cough as the air attacked his lungs. Chudamani covered his face to avoid any more surprise attack.

He walked around the city lines until he found his favorite spot in the city. His eyes stared at the massive reminder that there was once an empire that took on all challenges. His desire to stand just as sturdy as the Roman Colosseum was crumbling just like many other structures. It was time they took their sturdiness, but he refused.

"Admiring your own destiny, Chudamani?" A silky young woman's voice came.

He refused to look in her direction.

"Vicenzo told me you were rehearsing and that I would probably find you there. But I see his misguided nature remains, as here I am seeing you." She walked towards him.

Chudamani's gaze remained on the Colosseum, until she stood in front of him. Her dark, black hair was short, but it framed her oval face just right. Youth remained in the forty-something's face. Her figure was still straighter than a rail, even though she announced her two-month pregnancy.

"Nicola told me she saw you," she said. "She mentioned you looked well, that you were taking care of yourself and have someone new in your life. I'm glad."

"What do you care?" Chudamani snapped as he eyed his ex-fiancée. "You ran off for someone twenty years younger than me all because you didn't want to take care of an old man."

"I got scared."

"Bah, you didn't think you could handle what the future had for me. You thought I was done, Tazia! You saw a broken man, and you hated my dog too."

"That's not fair, Chudamani! I loved you, but I got scared when I saw you lying in that bed, lifeless! I spent days in the hospital, hoping you'd come back to me."

Chudamani stared at her, as the elegant woman placed her hand on her stomach. She still held some power over him, but he felt mocked that he wasn't the one who married her.

"Maybe you were afraid that I couldn't give you what you wanted, but I'm happy for you. Giacome should be proud that he knocked you up just after the wedding."

"How dare you!" Tazia slapped him across the face, knocking his sunglasses off. "You don't know the struggle I had to go through to get this baby! Don't act like you know what hell I've been through since I walked out that church in my dress. I made the choice because I was scared. I knew I wasn't ready to take care of anyone but a child."

He stared in the direction of his fallen sunglasses. His face throbbed from her powerful smack. Chudamani felt the full wrath of Tazia and could feel the anger that she held onto. He breathed deep as he kept his eye contact from her.

"And from what I see, you are seeing someone just as young…is she worth it, that American? Or did you decide to finally sleep with Pietra? That whore always got what she wanted; even your mother loved her."

"Pietra is hardly a part of this conversation, Tazia, and leave Danielle out of it as well."

"Do you love her, Chudamani? Do you want her to be the one who takes care of you as you slowly breakdown? Is she willing to put you back together when the time comes that you can no longer breathe on your own? Please, what kind of life is that?"

"Mine! It's my fucking life, Tazia!" He shouted. "I've accepted what I am, and if you can't then, please, leave me. Go to your fucking husband, and leave me the fuck alone!"

"Maybe that is what you want, Chudamani—to die alone. To curl up and die, just like your father, just like everyone in your life does. I'm glad I didn't marry you, and I'm glad you are suffering like I did for the three years we were together! Never knowing when you wouldn't wake up to see the sun again, or have a seizure on stage and fall!"

"You hate me; I get it!"

"I hate myself for leaving you! I hate you for almost dying!" Her voice wavered, as tears fell from her face.

He looked at her, and her perfect brow showed her age. She swallowed the lump in her throat and breathed.

"Hell, I've been in hell and punishing myself for leaving you! You were frail and barely standing six months ago, on the tip of falling over."

Chudamani closed his eyes, and he reached up to rub his head. He felt the string of pain stabbing his head. He reached into his pocket to find he had taken his medicine out of his pocket. He stood up, frantic, and Tazia looked at him with a worried expression. He staggered towards the direction of the stadium.

"Chudamani?" Tazia questioned.

His eyes were sensitive to the light, and he knew he needed to move quickly before he had an episode in public.

"Chudamani!" She rushed behind him and grabbed his arm. "Sit down, you fool!"

"No, I need to go." He became breathless as panic took control.

He stumbled, and Tazia grabbed him before he fell. She pulled her phone out and called for help.

"No, help get me to the stadium." He glared at her.

Chudamani's eyes fluttered, and a strong pain remained knocking on his head. He pulled away from her, and, without warning, threw up in the nearest bush.

"Chudamani?" Tazia questioned.

"I need to lay down," he said. "Get me to the stadium, now!"

Tazia called her driver to come pick them up. He remained hovered over the bush and thanked whoever saved him from having an episode in public.

"Here," Tazia said offering him a wipe.

"Is this a mother thing that you acquired being with Giacome? He's barely out of diapers."

"Still an asshole, even after throwing up." Tazia slapped his head.

He wiped his mouth and slowly stood straight, feeling the pain remain, but he would make sure he chewed his medicine.

"Here's the car," Tazia said as she grabbed his arm.

He walked, staggering slightly as he got in and breathed in deep to keep a calm composure. His eyes closed, and he tried to focus on happier things in his life. His thoughts fell away as the soothing car ride rocked him to sleep, despite the short time.

Once at the stadium, there was a greeting committee waiting for his arrival. Vicenzo and Natalia had promised to stop by to work on the duets they did on the new album.

"Well, look what the stray dogs dragged in," Vicenzo walked over to them. "The scrappy woman got her claws in you."

"Piss off, Vicenzo. He needs rest." Tazia looked at the fifty-something-year-old singer.

His surprise appeared on his face, and concern swept over as well for his half-awake friend.

"Get me medicine, Vicenzo; it's on my dressing room counter."

"You need to lay down. Let's go," Vicenzo said, knowing the weakened string of words.

Vicenzo looked at Natalia, as she walked over briskly.

"Thank you, Tazia," Natalia said. "He's grateful, but you should go."

"But…"

"Just go. You've done enough," Vicenzo snapped.

He walked Chudamani to his dressing room and hurried to get the medicine. He handed him a fresh bottle of water and the two white pills. Chudamani chewed the chalky medicine and sipped water. He found comfort on the hard sofa.

"Should I call Danielle?"

"No, let her have time to visit with family." Chudamani objected. "I just need sleep. Turn off the lights on your way out."

"Of course." Vicenzo walked towards the door. "For the record, I still hate Tazia."

"I do too." Chudamani muttered.

Vicenzo smiled and turned off the lights before he left, leaving Chudamani in darkness once again.

"Danielle, hello?" Tyler called as he waved his hand in front of her face.

Danielle blinked and looked over at her brother. He took a leave for a week to help sort things of their mother's.

"She left me with junk, Ty," Danielle said, staring at the nearly unbearable living situation.

"She was senile, Dani," Tyler answered as he cleaned up bedpans. "She did mention your name before she went to bed every night. I think she missed you. You never called her or even checked up."

"She never wanted me around. Harrison was the one she wanted, to show her son-in-law off to her friends. Daddy hated that people looked at us strangely when Harrison and I got married. He appreciated the idea of keeping it simple, but Mama, she wanted the best that Southern girls deserved."

Danielle sat down at the kitchen table and looked at Tyler, as he shuffled and threw out magazines their mother kept. He shook them, and money fell out of it. Danielle wrinkled her brow and walked over.

"Is that…?" Danielle asked.

"Oh, it is." Tyler knelt and lifted three, hundred-dollar bills. "What was she thinking?"

Danielle looked at the crisp hundreds and knelt. Tyler handed it to her.

"It's your junk now, but I take ten percent," he joked.

"Ten percent of total or every bill?" Danielle smiled.

"There's the smile I haven't seen since you got here." Tyler reached over to her. "Why do you hate it here so much? Why do you hate us?"

"I don't hate you, Ty. I just disliked how Mama thought of me as her saving grace to get out of this dirty parish. I don't blame her, but Harrison and I married for love, not for status. She used him to cash out of this fishing community. She pushed me on every rich man she could to help her cause."

"Maybe she wanted what was best for you, Dani. Mama never said what she believed, because her parents told her to raise us with an iron thumb." Tyler lifted other magazines and shook them to find more squirreled away money. "Shit, this is a lot of bucks!"

Danielle glanced out the window in the vast miles of fishing camps and the swampy land that the label told her she'd return to if she didn't get her job done.

"Ty?" Danielle asked.

"Yes?"

"Do you believe that there's a plan for our lives that we don't know about?"

Tyler sat down the pile of magazines and stared at her. She seemed like she was looking for permission to do something.

"I believe we have a plan for our lives that we make, that higher power thing was never my belief. Why?"

Danielle stood up and looked around the family home. The sturdy home survived fifteen hurricanes, two fires, and her mother's rampage after her father came clean with an affair. She never felt so safe in the house, but the storm that brewed in her didn't make her feel safe either. She was anxious to believe that the higher power could take so much away from her and then tease her with something else.

"I came here because you called about Mama, but everything I'm surrounded…I know this is not where I'm supposed to be." Danielle looked at Tyler.

"What are you talking about?" Tyler asked. "You are here because you belong here with your family, Dani. You flew here because you came to your senses."

"No, Ty, I came to pay my respects and fly back. I took a leave for a week to help and clear my head. I've been blind for so long because I believed my promise to Harrison would protect me from losing someone else. As you see, I lost Mama; I even lost you."

"How?"

"Because you don't believe I should be anywhere, but home, making babies and running a house. Mama may have been a crazy lady, but, maybe you were right, she was trying to get me away from the life she was stuck with. She craved adventure like I did and didn't know how to tell me." Danielle looked at Tyler. "You joined the Air Force for what reason?"

"So, I could protect my country." Tyler looked at her.

"Company man," Danielle said. "Always, the company line. But you really wanted to get away from here, from this life. You were happy to be at least out of this fishing community."

Danielle stared at the magazines, and the travel magazines, the cruises that her mother wanted to take. She was scratching to get out and live a life outside from under her father's own iron thumb. She served her father like a loyal house wife would do, but it wasn't her. She was so full of life when she talked about going to other states with her family. Going to college to be a professor was her greatest achievement until she got pregnant.

"I'm not going to be like Mama and go out in a wooden box. I'm going to live where I need to be."

"Damn it, Dani! Stop with these stupid ideas that you belong in that country! You are a fucking American and the daughter of a fisherman and house wife. You ain't nothing more than that. That country has poisoned your head with ideas! I'd be damned, as head of this family, to let you go back!"

Danielle nodded, collected the magazines, and shoved them in a box. She lifted it up and stuffed them in the back of her father's pick-up truck.

"I'm at the Daisy Inn if you want to understand what's on my mind." Danielle smiled. "So, Ty, love you, but please fuck off."

She walked out the door and got into the truck. There was something so freeing about telling her brother to 'fuck off' and then drive away. She sped down the road and made her way to the motel.

The screaming crowd chanted for the talented three that came together to show that they stood in a category of their own. Natalia, Vicenzo, and Chudamani rushed the stage as they brought back their classic set, adding flare to each of their own sets.

"The beautiful Natalia Laterza!" Chudamani presented her and kissed her cheek.

"My brother, separated at birth, Vicenzo Scordato!"

Vicenzo walked up and took a bow before hugging Chudamani. He lifted his microphone and looked to Natalia as she walked up.

"Chudamani Amoretto!" They both presented him.

"Grazie, tutti!" The three pointed to the crowd.

They stepped back, and the band played a little. Chudamani hugged Natalia and kissed her cheek.

"Have you heard from Danielle?" Natalia asked.

They grabbed a towel and dabbed away the sweat. Chudamani shook his head and grabbed an ice-cold bottle of water.

"She's mourning for her mother…It was best I leave her alone." Chudamani leaned against an amp.

"She needs her friend," Natalia said. "Someone that believes what she does here is for the best."

Chudamani placed his index and middle finger on his neck as he checked his pulse. He could feel the excitement was part of the racing beat, but he felt something was wrong.

"She told me about the kiss," Natalia mentioned.

"The what?" Vicenzo questioned. "Did you finally sleep with her?"

"Sleep with her! Have some respect, you ass!" Natalia slapped him on the back of the head. "She's a woman, not a piece of meat you order off a menu. Wait until I tell Angelica."

Vicenzo gave Natalia a look before glancing over at Chudamani, who lightly wiped the sweat off the back of his neck and sighed.

"And what did she tell you, because she did not tell me anything. I was just as surprised as she was when she kissed me."

"Awe, did you do the little school boy giggle?" Vicenzo teased.

Chudamani splashed Vicenzo with the water as they both laughed.

"You two are idiots." Natalia shook her head.

The two of them walked over to her and kissed her cheek. She wrinkled her nose, as she pushed them away and wiped their own sweat off her.

"She's like our little sister," Vicenzo mentioned. "I love you, Natalia, even with your belief that your sweat doesn't smell."

"Manly sweat isn't as nice as mine."

Chudamani smiled and swatted both with the towel, and all youth came to the three singers as they forgot the topic at hand.

"Natalia, Vicenzo, Chudamani, you're on for one more," the stage manager said.

The three of them nodded and took a breath. Vicenzo rushed onto stage, as the band began to play a song that would appear on all three of their albums. Natalia looked at Chudamani and patted his cheek.

"She's hurting too. Her husband died, and she lost her child two months after him. She believes she's being mocked about being here with you. Maybe it's time to show her that it isn't true." Natalia smiled and walked with such elegance back onstage.

Chudamani took a deep breath and hurried onto the stage to make his cue. The energy of the crowd fed their excitement. Chudamani jumped down and walked between the space of the stage and the floor seating.

Vicenzo and Natalia followed his out-of-the-box thinking and walked to their next point.

A final bow was made, and they left the stage. Chudamani walked down the corridor to his dressing room to find an unexpected visitor.

"Hello, Chudamani," Pietra greeted him.

"Pietra," he said.

The elegant woman walked over and kissed his cheek. She was dressed for a formal event and seemed rather upset about something. Her painted lips pressed hard together.

"I wanted to be at your concert tonight, but I had other obligations," Pietra said as she walked over to the counter in his dressing room.

"I'm not surprised; you are the label head's daughter. You have your obligations to appear often in public."

"Yes, that is true. And you know who I ran into while I was sporting my million-euro smile?"

Chudamani looked at her, as her hand rested on the prescription bottle. She looked at him, using his reflection.

"I bet you will tell me who," Chudamani remarked.

"My dear friend and nurse at the hospital. She gave valuable information on the superstar Chudamani Amoretto. It is funny what can be up for the highest bid." Pietra turned her gaze to him.

She walked towards him and tossed the medicine bottle. She also lifted the white card that he normally kept in his wallet.

"It makes sense, now, as to why you have that mongrel."

Chudamani stiffened and raised his gaze to meet her form, which was much too close to his.

"She's not a mongrel; she's my companion."

"You silly, silly man," Pietra said as she dragged the white card up his chest. "Did you really think my father would let this…whatever it is, go on under his nose?"

Chudamani stared at the flawless face before him. She knew how to use her charm to exploit information, like a spy getting intel. He grabbed the card from her, and she lightly stroked his cheek.

"What do you want, Pietra?" Chudamani asked.

"Don't you know?" Pietra whispered in his ear.

Her other hand grabbed him, and he choked at her iron grasp. She smiled and pressed her painted red lips on his cheek.

"Clean up before you come over. I like my guests to be cleaned."

"I'm not sleeping with you." Chudamani stared at her.

"You're not? Then I suggest you find yourself a new label. I can change my father's mind if you change yours." Pietra looked at him.

She smiled at him as she walked away. He waited until she left the room and cursed as he reached for a cool bottle of water.

"Bitch." He sat down on the sofa.

Vicenzo opened the door and looked at him. "I can come back if you need a moment."

"Piss off." He threw a nearby towel.

"Pietra Ferrari just walked out here, dressed," Vicenzo mentioned. "How did that go down?"

"She got her giggles by grabbing my balls in her iron-clad hand." Chudamani pointed to the water bottle.

"Painful, but tolerable."

Vicenzo walked over and sat down, looking at the not-so-pleased face of his friend. Chudamani slapped him in the back of his head.

"She knows. Some nurse squealed, and she's blackmailing me." Chudamani stood up but decided it wasn't for the best.

"I take back using Danielle as your getting-back-on-the-horse—go for her. Bang her once and go home. Better than having *that* happen every time she needs leverage."

"Angelica must have been drugged when she married you. She'd beat you senseless if she heard you talk so disgusting." Chudamani raised his brow at him. "I'm not going over there, because I'm not giving that power to her. The label already knows."

"But she can go public," Vicenzo said.

"And maybe it's time." Chudamani finally stood up. "I'm tired of hiding this. Lots of people are worse off than me, and they still dance and sing. My condition can be controlled—less stress, more exercise."

"More sex will help you."

"I swear."

"What?"

"I can produce if I don't have a music career. I can work boards and help mentor others. There are plenty of things I can do. Hiding is not one thing."

Vicenzo's eyes became wide, and he raised his hands and clapped. Chudamani shook his head.

"You realize you are not the same man. I've seen you tell people to fuck off when they insulted your music. I've seen you walk onstage, drunk off your ass. But never have I seen you admit that you were ready to come clean. She really did a number on you, didn't she?"

"Fuck off, Vicenzo! No one has done a number on me. I'm just tired of this bullshit. Maybe Fiorella is right, that I do have an expiration date. And maybe it is a lot sooner than I thought."

"Fuck that shit! You're not retiring from this."

Vicenzo grabbed Chudamani's arm, and he wrinkled his brow.

"You're my brother. When I had that drinking problem early in my career, you dragged me to get help. Met my ex-wife, but still dragged me. You made me stay at your place until I was dried out. You stuffed pills down my throat to remind me it was a sickness, not my life. God, I love you, Chudamani, because you helped me find Angelica. I was a sad sack of something. So, I'm going to do the same. You are not alone in this fight."

"I love you like a brother, Vicenzo, but sometimes the towel needs to be thrown in."

"Like hell it does!" Vicenzo pointed at him. "Watch what I can do. I'm about to drop a miracle on you."

"You are a fucking moron, Vicenzo," Chudamani laughed.

"Just wait, bring the storm."

Chudamani shook his head as his crazy friend walked out. He walked to the counter and stared at a tired fifty-something-year-old. He brushed the more-than-stubble, dark hair on his head. He had gotten lucky that the grey had not touched his head. He still felt like he'd lose all his dignity after his treatment, but his color was still there.

He smiled and took two more pills before jumping into the shower. Chudamani took the time to rinse away the sweat and the idea that Pietra had some power over his career. He scrubbed hard, as he felt dirty for even playing with the idea to give the label what they wanted.

As he walked out, he grabbed a towel and wrapped it around his waist. His hand rushed over the steamed mirror, where he saw the reminder of his surgery. The scar remained where they cut to get to the tumor. His hand lightly traced the skin toned scar to feel the raised skin remained. He took several deep breaths as he tried to hold back the pain. He wasn't alone, but there were times he felt alone.

"You can't give up easily, you old bastard," he muttered. "You still got your looks, and your spirit is building back up."

Chudamani nodded and went off to dress before he would leave the stadium. It wasn't easy for him to stare at himself in a mirror and see how his life had changed because of a cut down his chest.

He walked out, zipping up his jacket.

"Hello, stranger," a young woman's voice said.

He turned and looked at the young woman. She was dressed for a night out, high boots and a short dress.

"So, you're *that* guy," she said.

"I am." He smiled at the lady of the night.

"Buy a girl a cup of coffee?" She asked.

"Sure, should I call my brother, so he can hear your confession?" Chudamani asked.

She smiled, and he presented his arm to her. She walked over and slipped her arm around his.

"How did you find me?"

"The same way I find all my clients. I look for the saddest looking man and ask if he wants company."

"Oh, so you are a lady of the night with a heart?" He joked with the young woman.

She shook her head as they walked towards the café not far from the stadium. He pulled her chair out for her, then sat down. The delicate woman strutted a tough look, but he could see there was a lost soul too. The bruises on her cheek were not disguised enough by the make-up. Her weak grasp around his arm suggested maybe a broken wrist.

"So, the wife was just an excuse to turn me down with dignity? She asked.

"It took a lot of will power to do so. You seemed like someone in my old life I'd gladly say yes to, though I never paid."

"Of course, because it came easy to you. You flash that smile, and women just swoon over you. You ask them to sleep with you, and they just take you up."

Chudamani laughed a little and nodded. "That's about it."

"What does Father Francis say about your younger days?" She asked as she leaned back in the iron back chair. "Is he ashamed?"

"I stopped because of one woman I loved. She was and aspiring model and gorgeous, even though she had a hard time adjusting to the lifestyle. Met her on my video and we hit it off. We fell in love and lived life how we should, but then I got sick. I had a tumor on my left lung, ended up being cancerous. I went for treatment and reacted to it badly. I was in a coma for almost a year. They said there was nothing wrong, and now I live with the possibilities of episodic seizures. She left me at the altar, not wanting to take care of me for the rest of her life." Chudamani explained to the young woman.

"You poor thing," she said. "I think you need something stronger than coffee."

"Wish I could partake in that, but I can't even have that."

"What do you do?"

"I found a life that suited me, moved out of Rome and live in a place where its quiet. I have a translator who stays with me, but she's left to take care of family."

The young woman reached for his hand and lifted it to her lips.

"I don't see a broken man. I see someone who takes their licks and gets going." Her ice-blue gaze seemed to sparkle a little. "You just need someone to understand what you are doing. Someone who has a familiar story."

"Now, you sound like my brother. He's got this whole idea that I'm following a path that will lead me to happiness, but I think happiness is long gone."

The young woman glanced out and pointed to the city.

"Do you believe that the Romans gave up building an empire when they were attacked every time? Or the Pope gives up his faith when a crisis against Christians happens?"

"No." Chudamani shook his head.

"Then you shouldn't give up on happiness because something was thrown in your path. You just find a new way to get there. It may be long and hard, but, believe me, you will find your happiness."

She glanced at the golden watch on her right wrist and stood up. She walked over and kissed his cheek.

"If you ever need a friend, I'll be around." She winked at him.

"What is your name?"

"Speranza," she answered.

She gave a back handed wave and walked out into the streets. He watched her catch a taxi and get in. He smiled and glanced over to see she left a calling card. He chuckled and stuffed it in his back pocket.

CHAPTER NINE

Each day seemed like he was sitting on the edge of his seat. He was expecting a notice that he would be dropped from his label, so his trying to keep the stress down was becoming an issue. He had no buffer except Portia. It was becoming hard to control his migraines, which normally were signs that he could possibly have a seizure and not a small one.

His eyes stared at the weary-looking face in the mirror. He slowly shaved away the heavy scruff until he was nearly baby-face smooth. He smiled and looked over at Portia, as she seemed on edge as well.

"What do you think? Does it say, 'I'm trying'?" Chudamani asked.

She barked and wagged her tail at him. He chuckled and walked to the shower to start the water. He walked out, and he rubbed Portia's heavy coat.

"I miss her too, girl," he said.

She licked his hand, and he kissed her head. "She'll be back, I promise. She's got to keep me on my toes and piss me off somehow."

She barked at him, making him smile.

"We all need a little time to find where we are in life." His gaze was soft as he stared out in the direction of the window.

Portia pawed at him because his hand stopped petting her. Her bark became a panic and a yelp. It was then that his eyes rolled back, and he fell forward seizing.

It was the panic bark that was heard to alert someone down the hall. With the turn of the key, the door opened.

"Chudamani!" A panicked voice came.

As the seizure passed, he laid there to allow his body to fully relax. The gentle strokes on his back were felt as he slowly sat up and threw up. He coughed as he choked up, leaning forward until he could breathe past the constant bile coming up.

"Here, water," Vicenzo's voice came beside his saving aid.

"Drink." An ivory hand reached around to hand him the cup of water.

His eyes stared at the hand, and he grabbed it.

"Danielle," he whispered.

Chudamani turned and looked at her, as she smiled and nodded. He pushed himself up and took the cup to wash away the horrible residue from throwing up. Danielle lightly rubbed his back.

"Is he alright?" Natalia's voice asked.

"He's going to be fine." Danielle stared at the dazed look in his eyes. "But he's not out of the woods yet."

Natalia walked over and grabbed a cloth to hand to Danielle. She gently wiped away the evidence from his face and on the floor. He turned his gaze away. She grabbed his hand and lightly stroked it.

"He's probably groggy; he should lay down." Vicenzo knelt beside them. "Hey, buddy, let's get you off the floor."

Danielle slowly stood, and Vicenzo helped Chudamani to stand. He guided him to the bed and let him lay down on his own. Danielle patted the bed, and Portia curled up beside him. She licked his face and tucked herself under his arms.

"I'll stay with him," Danielle said.

"His medication is by the sink. He's going to need it right away," Natalia said giving Danielle's shoulder a pat.

Vicenzo looked at her and Danielle gave a weak smile.

"Thank you, Vicenzo, for calling me." Danielle walked over to him and hugged him. "I needed the reason to get here quicker."

He smiled and leaned his head on hers, embracing her tightly. Natalia looked at Chudamani, who fell asleep without a problem.

"What about the show tonight?" Natalia asked.

"He can't perform; that seizure took all he had." Danielle glanced over.

"We'll take care of it." Vicenzo patted her cheek. "We're professionals."

Danielle nodded, and Natalia hugged her.

"I'm glad you are back; you are good for him." Natalia smiled.

As the hours ticked away, Danielle curled up in a chair by the window with a good book. She flipped the pages and glanced up to see him still sleeping. She sighed and walked over to see Portia had moved to the edge of the bed. She petted Portia's head and thanked her for being there for him.

"You came back," Chudamani mumbled.

Danielle glanced up and saw him open his eyes. She smiled and nodded to his comment.

"I came back." Danielle sat on the edge of the bed. "I didn't belong there."

Chudamani slowly turned over and stared at her. She was different in his eyes. There was something there he just couldn't explain.

"Could you lay down with me?" He asked with a groggy voice. "I promise I won't pull anything."

Danielle smiled and walked over to the empty side of the bed. She knelt into the comforts and crawled in beside him. She slid close to him and faced him. He tucked his arm under his head as he looked into her eyes. She reached up and stroked the groomed facial hair that circled his lips with a thin line outlined his jaw.

It was the first time they just laid in bed together where Danielle felt it was so natural. It was a peaceful feeling that calmed her cluttered mind. He reached over and lightly stroked her cheek.

"I've missed you," he whispered.

"I missed you too." Danielle smiled.

There was a glimmer of sadness that dripped from her eyes. He reached up and wiped away the moisture that slid down her blushed cheeks. It scared her to see him in such a helpless condition, but she stayed with him every step of the way. He leaned towards her and touched his forehead to hers.

"Please, don't cry. I'm here still." He smiled.

"I'm sorry," she whispered. "I was scared that I could have lost you."

"I don't plan to go anywhere."

She took a deep breath, and he stroked her cheek. He pulled her close to him and held her as she began to cry. It was that moment when all the feelings that were there were finally released. He closed his eyes, feeling the sadness leave him. He never wanted to show anyone the life he now had to deal with, but, as he showed more, she stayed.

"Please, don't go back," he choked on his tears.

"No, I'm not going back," she said as she nestled closer to him.

"I missed you so much, Danielle. I couldn't sleep without knowing you were here." Chudamani closed his eyes tighter as more tears slipped down his face.

While another hour passed, Danielle held him in her arms. She stroked his head and listened to his breathing. His strong arms were wrapped around her torso, and he slept with ease for the first time.

A soft knock on the door alerted Portia, and she glanced at the sleeping man, not wanting to wake him.

"Danielle," Antonio's voice came through the door.

"Come in," she called lightly.

The sound of a key being turned made Portia muff. She got up and sat at the door, waiting for it to open.

"Portia, it is only me," he said, patting her. "Where is our patient?"

She got up and jumped back on the bed. He walked over and stared at the sleeping man, as he held Danielle.

"I see he wasted no time to get you in bed," the older man softly laughed.

"With my clothes on," Danielle remarked as she continued to stroke Chudamani's head. "Is there something you needed?"

Antonio pulled out the contract and Danielle sighed.

"He needs to sign it now before Pietra gabs and before this gets out." Antonio looked at her. "You are the only one he will listen too. Vicenzo and Natalia tried, but he won't sign it."

Danielle reached for it, and Chudamani stirred a little. She lightly stroked his head again as she put the contract to the side.

"I've made arrangements for another show tomorrow. He'll make that won't he?"

"I'll make sure."

"Keep doing what you do for him, Danielle. You've become a valuable asset."

"I hope more than that?"

"I think so." He smiled and walked towards the door. "Keep him safe."

Danielle listened for the door and looked down at Chudamani.

The next day, the winter rain came baring its teeth down on the Roman city. Danielle found comfort in her book, while Chudamani read over the contract again. She could see that he was frustrated with the wording, tossing the pen. She looked over her book as he removed the black framed glasses he was instructed to wear when reading.

"I'm already on the chopping block," he mentioned.

"You are hardly on the chopping block, Chudamani. You have a chance for a new beginning."

"They are saying they can end my contract if I cancel six shows. So, in other words, if I have a series of seizures and cancel any of those shows, I'm done." Chudamani glanced over at her. "They are treating me like I'm expired."

"Then prove to them you aren't," Danielle said as she closed her book. "Go to every show and tailor it to how you feel you need to."

Danielle reached over and grabbed his hand. She lightly stroked it, and he lifted her hand to his lips.

"That's enough of this; we're going for a walk." She grabbed her jacket.

"It's raining and cold." He gave a confused look.

"So? The cold never bothered you before."

"I'm a little sore from falling on the floor." He made an excuse.

She reached behind her and handed him the aspirin. He wrinkled his nose, and she shrugged.

"I'm tired of being cooped up in this room until the show." She walked over to him and grabbed his hand. "Don't be a sour puss."

"Oh, I'm the sour puss? What about you when you wouldn't go with me to get new clothes, but you'd go with Natalia?"

She rolled her eyes and pulled at him to get up from the chair. He pulled back, and she stumbled but kept her fight.

"Come on, old man," she teased.

"Old man? Old man? That was a hit below the belt, little girl." He stuck his tongue out at her.

"Man child." She laughed. "Come on, Portia needs to get out."

Portia barked at them as they teased each other. She jumped up on Danielle and pushed her towards Chudamani. Danielle stumbled and fell right into his arms. She blinked slightly, as he swept her into his arms and threw her over his shoulder.

"Hey, you can't do that!" Danielle laughed.

He reached up and gave her butt a pat, and she swatted him back. "That just doesn't have the same effect on men, signora."

"Really?"

"Nope," he chuckled. "Come on, Portia."

Portia barked and followed her master as he carried Danielle. He carried her down the hall and stopped at one room. He hit on the wooden door.

"Come on, Vicenzo," Chudamani called.

Vincenzo walked out tucking his shirt in. "Do you mind? I do have a wife to keep happy."

"Gross!" Danielle expressed with great repulsion.

"Why is she over your shoulder like that? Is this some kinky thing you're trying?"

"Gross, Vicenzo, is sex always on your brain?" Danielle looked over.

"When I'm in the mood. What do you want?"

"Zip up and grab your *real* guitar, not the *thing* you call a guitar." Chudamani looked at his friend. "Hi, Angelica!"

"Hi, Chudamani," the Italian actress peeked from behind the door.

"I like my *thing* I call a guitar!" Vicenzo called as they walked on.

Chudamani knocked on three doors in a row, and his band stuck their heads out.

"Grab your gear and meet me downstairs." Chudamani looked at them. "Wake Natalia up, and tell her to warm up her vocals."

He walked on, and Danielle sighed as he still carried her.

"Still with me?" Chudamani asked.

"I can't go anywhere." She swatted at him again.

"Still nothing," Chudamani remarked.

He carried her down to the lobby floor and looked at the restaurant full of people. He smiled and went to the desk clerk.

"Where can I set up for an impromptu show?" He asked.

"Ah, you can use the lobby." The desk clerk pointed.

He gave a nod, and his band walked down along with Natalia and Vicenzo. Both looked at him weirdly, as he still carried Danielle over his shoulder.

"She's not your rag doll, Chudamani," Natalia mentioned.

"You're right." Chudamani slightly tossed her and caught her in his arms. "She's so much more."

Danielle looked at him as he smiled. He sat her down and patted her on the butt, and she shook her head.

"Ass."

"I am what I am." Chudamani folded his arms.

As soon as the band set up, Chudamani looked at his two closest friends and smiled. The first notes filled the lobby of the five-star hotel with a familiar song. People stopped and watched as the three singers welcomed the crowd in their impromptu acoustic session.

What seemed like a few quickly became many, as more guests came down and began to film it. Danielle watched as a renewed spirit showed in Chudamani's eyes. Her gaze looked over at Angelica, as the Italian actress smiled at her husband. She walked over to her and finally introduced herself.

"It is a pleasure to finally meet you," Angelica stated. "Vicenzo told me so much about what you do for Chudamani. I think he's different now."

"I do too."

"You are so much better than that other woman, Tazia. She was too selfish for her own good." Angelica rolled her eyes. "And that other woman, Pietra, she blackmailed him to sleep with her."

"What?"

"You didn't hear about that?" Angelica folded her arms. "Vicenzo told me. She was in his dressing room and found his medication. That woman is something else. It's because her father owns the label he's on. She's only been trying to sleep with him for four years."

Danielle looked at Angelica with irritation as she suddenly felt that Chudamani slept with Pietra. She looked over at him.

"She's a slut," Danielle muttered.

"I agree, but she's good at her job of manipulating people."

"Did he sleep with her?"

"Heaven's no! He wouldn't go near that whore."

Danielle slightly sighed, and Angelica rested her hand on her shoulder.

"He's got someone else on his mind," Angelica said with a smile.

Danielle felt herself blush, as she glanced over at Chudamani. He looked over in her direction at the same moment and winked. Danielle shook her head, as he shrugged and smirked.

He walked through the crowd and danced with a guest. She laughed, as he knelt to her level and the girl took a selfie. He moved through and kissed an old lady's cheek. Chudamani eventually made his way to sing right in front of Danielle. She pushed him away, but he grabbed her hand.

"Go out with me," he said.

"No," she said playfully.

"I won't move," he said to her.

"You'll miss your cue."

"Vicenzo will pick it up." He grabbed her hand and pulled her to the front.

She felt her cheeks become warm as he pulled her to the front. She felt herself become nervous.

"Should this lovely lady go out with me?" He asked.

There were plenty who shouted 'yes' to him.

"Should I kiss her?" Chudamani looked at her.

"Don't." Danielle smiled.

"The public has spoken." He smiled slyly and pulled her to him, dipping her for a kiss.

The crowd went wild as he kissed her, and she wrapped her arms around him. A feeling of complete bliss escaped their lips.

"I told you I missed you," Chudamani said.

"You ass." Danielle smiled and shook her head.

Chudamani kissed her hand and let her go back to standing in the back. She laughed while the crowd clapped for her.

"I told you he had someone else on his mind." Angelica smiled.

Danielle laughed, feeling that was the only thing she could do. Portia sat beside Chudamani, as they returned to a softer song.

###

That night at the show, Chudamani returned to his routine of meditation. He calmed his breaths and let his heart beat softly. The anxiety in his chest was relieved as he channeled a hopefulness that his future would bring him a brighter report.

A soft knock on the door pulled him from his thoughts. He looked at the door with one eye open.

"Chudamani," Danielle's voice came.

"Come in." He returned to meditating.

The door opened, and Danielle walked in. He opened his eyes and looked at her to see that she held something in her hand.

"What is that?" Chudamani asked.

"Nothing important." Danielle walked into the dressing room.

She knelt in front of him and handed him two white pills.

"Take your medicine. I'm still concerned about that last episode. You are still tired, and I want you to be at your best." Danielle reached over and stroked his cheek.

"Come sit with me." He patted the ground beside him.

She walked over and sat down beside him. She crossed her legs at her ankle, and he looked at her ankle to see a butterfly tattoo. He put one arm around her shoulder leaned his head on hers.

"What is the tattoo for?" He asked.

Danielle looked down at it and pulled down the black leggings over her ankle.

"It's a memory." She looked at him.

"What memory?" Chudamani placed his hand on her cheek.

Danielle stared at him and leaned her head against his.

"I had a child once," Danielle confessed.

"Once?"

"Yes, she was born two months early with a weak heart. They thought they could do surgery and save her, but she died on the operating table." Danielle felt her lower lip quiver.

He pulled her into his arms, and she wrapped her arms tightly around him.

"I'm sorry; I didn't mean to bring this up." He ran his hands through her auburn locks. "I could not imagine what that is like, losing a child."

"I thought things couldn't get worse after Harrison was killed, but, to lose the other piece of him, I found out how much it did." Danielle closed her eyes tightly as tears fell. "I got the tattoo the week I was leaving for Italy to carry the memory of her."

"What was her name?"

"Josephine Maria Bennet. I had her baptized before she went into surgery, hoping that would save her."

Chudamani kissed her head, as he heard the subtle sobs escape her lips. He could not heal the loss of a child, but he could comfort her. His selfishness of being the wounded bird blinded him from her pain, despite her confession of the loss of her husband. He did not pry or want to pry because it was her life.

"That is a beautiful name for a child." Chudamani kissed her head.

He knew there was a song he could sing and help maybe ease her pain.

"Do you have a picture?" He asked.

"Of her?"

"Yes."

Danielle nodded and reached for her phone and pulled up the picture. Chudamani stared at the happy mother and beautiful baby. He smiled and looked at her as she stared at the memory before her.

"And your husband?"

Danielle slid to the picture of Harrison in his camo. Chudamani felt a little jealous that this man kept Danielle's heart even after death. But he ignored the jealousy and sent both pictures to his phone.

"What are you doing?" Danielle asked in confusion.

"I'm going to dedicate this show to them." Chudamani kissed her head. "Because you care so much for them, I'm going to let my fans know they are important to the people I care about."

Danielle wrapped her arms around him tightly, and he hugged her back.

Chudamani walked down the corridor holding Danielle's hand, kissing that back of it after guiding her towards the side of the stage. He slipped the ear piece in and took a deep breath, tossing his phone to a stagehand. He informed them when to put the pictures up.

"Tonight, they will never be forgotten," he told her.

"Thank you," she whispered, sniffling.

He walked onstage with strength to his vocals. His energy was high, despite recovering from a grand-mal seizure. His very movements were as if his body had rebooted itself and kicked up his energy level.

"He's on fire!" Vicenzo came up from behind.

"He is," Danielle replied.

Vicenzo looked at her and slightly put his arm around her. He kissed her head, and she smiled.

"He's a mess, Danielle, but I think you can handle that mess better," Vicenzo mentioned to her. "He wouldn't have let you stay for as long as he did if he didn't trust you can handle the situation he was in."

Danielle's gaze fell to the energy the crowd was giving off. She smiled and looked at Vicenzo again.

"How is he, really?" Danielle asked.

"What do you mean?"

"Since all this started? He seems fine, but his label wouldn't be so concerned about him with a new contract."

Vicenzo frowned and took a deep breath.

"It is my understanding that the damage done will affect him later. He is just doing what he loves to do for that time." Vicenzo looked at her. "We all break down—some of us faster than others."

Danielle looked at Chudamani as he pointed upward to the seating area.

"Vicenzo, he's getting ready for the next song." A stage hand walked over.

"Grazie." Vicenzo nodded.

He gave her shoulder a squeeze and ran on stage to hype up the crowd. She smiled at the two best friends as they joked around onstage. It was refreshing to know he wasn't alone in the new world of music; he had two friends that kept each other ground and hyped.

As the last lucky fan left from meeting the trio of friends backstage, Chudamani, Vincenzo, and Natalia walked down the corridor, ready to clean up. Danielle walked on stage and sat on the edge of it to listen to the silence. Her gaze stared out, imagining herself with Harrison and enjoying the concert.

"It's time to let go, Dani, " She heard his voice beside her.

Danielle turned her head and stared at the broad-shouldered man. His thick beard and sun-tan made him look more fitting for the environment he was in. She reached over and rushed her hand through his dark, thick head of hair.

"I miss you so much," Danielle whispered. "I wish you were here, seeing all this."

He chuckled and grabbed her hand into his. "I am here."

"Where?"

"In the music you love, the words you hear." Harrison stood up. "I remember you made me listen to their music over and over, so I was able to recite it."

Danielle laughed and stared at the scruff she hated on him, but that was what she pictured every time she imagined him there with her.

"I decided to keep the beard and be the wolfman you always teased me about." He stroked her cheek. "You know, he's not so bad after all. I've been watching him, and he looks at you like you hung the sun and moon in the sky. He even stood up to your jackass brother. I tell you, Dani, I loved your family, but your brother was a chauvinistic asshole. He expected you to give up everything to take care of your mother."

Danielle nodded as she took his hand. He slipped his arm around her waist and took her hand, then dipped her to kiss her. She reached up and kissed him like she did that evening before he was deployed.

"It's time to let go, Dani. I'm with you, always. Look around you, and you'll see me. You'll feel me holding you at night. I'll whisper words of comfort in your ear. I'll kiss you and run my fingers through your auburn locks." He lifted her up in his arms. "Be the sunshine for the one that needs it now."

She gazed into his green eyes and stroked the thick beard. He leaned towards her and leaned his head on hers.

"I love you, Sunshine, always," he said.

Harrison sat her down and smiled.

"Danielle?" Chudamani's voice came from behind.

Danielle opened her eyes and stared into the empty stadium. She turned, meeting his hazel eyes. He held her coat for her as he waited, dressed to go out into the cold. She walked over to him, and he helped her put the coat on.

"Ready to go back to the hotel?" He asked.

Danielle gave a nod and wrapped her arm around his. They walked out together and waited for a car to pick them up. Her blue eyes stared up into the night sky, and she felt the fresh, brisk air on the clear evening.

"Danielle," Chudamani said.

Danielle glanced over and saw him standing by a car. She walked over as he put out his hand to her. She took his gloved hand and jumped into the warm car. He followed in and closed the door behind him.

"Vicenzo and Angelica already went back to the hotel?" Danielle asked.

"I think they were in a hurry to finish something we interrupted," Chudamani mentioned.

"You mean *you* interrupted." Danielle smiled.

"Well, you were guilty by association."

The ten-minute drive back to the hotel was quiet. She glanced over at Chudamani, as he stared out the window. His gaze was distant, but there was peace in it. Her gaze moved out the window on her side, and she watched as many people still walked around, despite the chill in the air. There was something peaceful, yet sad about the winter; she loved it.

As they approach the hotel, they saw a crowd standing outside. He looked over at Danielle, who seemed curious about this.

"Stay close to me." Chudamani smiled.

The driver got out and so did Chudamani. He stood to the side and helped her out of the car. She watched as screaming fans began to crowd them. He quickly signed autographs and took pictures, but he kept a hold on Danielle's hand.

Security came and guided them through the tight crowd, getting them quickly to the elevators. Chudamani pulled Danielle in before the doors closed. He chuckled and removed his sock knit cap. She smiled, and he looked at her as she shook her head.

"This is the life I have chosen." Chudamani shrugged.

"Does this happen often?"

"It happens more here than most places." He stepped closer to her. "They are harmless."

Danielle stared up at him, and he slipped his arm around her waist. He pulled her tightly to him and kissed her. The kiss that was way overdue between them since the first time he kissed her in the piazza. She reached up and wrapped her arms around him, and he pressed the emergency stop on the elevator to give them a moment.

She took a breath, and he pulled her back for another kiss. For the first time, she pushed back the memory of her husband. All the sadness vanished away for her.

He took a breath and smiled, as they resumed their ride up to the room. He led her to the hotel room and unlocked the door. Chudamani stopped in the doorway and swept her into his arms, carrying her across the threshold of the hotel room, like a groom carrying in his new bride.

The door shut behind them for the night.

CHAPTER TEN

The next morning, Chudamani heard the annoying ringtone he set up for the label. He reached for it, but the device stopped ringing. He moaned and got comfortable, holding the only person he wanted in his bed. His hazel gaze watched as she slept peacefully beside him. He turned to his side and pulled her close to him, listening to her gentle breathing.

It was then that there was a knock on the door, making Portia bark. He opened his eyes and grabbed his pants, before answering the door. Portia ran to the door, and Chudamani followed behind his anxious dog.

He opened door and stared at Vicenzo, who was standing there on the other side.

"It's eight thirty," Chudamani muttered.

"Yeah, and I thought you two should see this," Vicenzo responded.

Chudamani looked over his shoulder and back at him. Vicenzo wrinkled his brow, before he smiled a devilish smile.

"You two finally slept together?" Vicenzo whispered.

"Don't make a big deal about it," Chudamani said through gritted teeth.

"Was Portia in the same room?"

"Where what I suppose to put her?" Chudamani folded his arms.

Vicenzo knelt and petted Portia.

"Your poor dog heard *all* those noises you haven't heard in a long time."

"Real subtle." Chudamani rolled his eyes at Vicenzo as he petted Portia.

Vicenzo looked at his watch and looked at Chudamani.

"Skip pillow talk and take a shower together; that's fun too."

"It's not my first time, Vicenzo." Chudamani shook his head. "Goodbye, come back later."

He closed the door on Vicenzo and walked back to bed. He walked over to his side and just laid back down. He ran his hands through her hair while she slept and leaned over to kiss her cheek.

"Mi hai salvato," he whispered in her ear.

When Danielle finally woke up, Chudamani had fallen back to sleep. She turned to see him sleeping peacefully. She leaned to him and stroked his cheek. He smiled as he grabbed her hand and brought it to his lips.

"Buongiorno," he greeted her.

"Buongiorno," she greeted him in return.

His hazel eyes stared up at her blue-eyed gaze. He slipped his arm around her and sat up to kiss her. She smiled as he held her tight to him.

"Was someone at the door?" Danielle asked.

"An hour ago, yes. Vicenzo came to show us something, but I shooed him off." Chudamani kissed her. "We have the morning off."

She kissed him as he took her in his arms and laid her in the comforts of the bed. She stared up at him with a smile.

"What do you want to do?" Chudamani asked.

"Stay wrapped up in your arms." She reached up and stroked his cheek.

"That can be arranged."

The sound of her phone ringing made her groan in irritation. She told him to ignore it and continue to do what he was about to.

His phone rang again, and he groaned.

"Ignore it." Danielle stared at him.

"It's the label."

"They can wait; we have time." Danielle patted his cheek.

"You're right," he said.

But it was hard to ignore when the phones continued to ring. Both reached for their phones, and Danielle saw urgent messages from Fiorella.

"Fiorella called me," Danielle said.

"The label left me a message." Chudamani showed the voicemail icon.

Danielle slid open her text and a video popped up. She gasped at the video and showed Chudamani.

"What the…"

"That footage is from last night."

"In the elevator," Danielle added.

"There's more." Chudamani got a text from Natalia.

Danielle looked over his shoulder as breaking entertainment news played. She watched in horror, as a statement from the label could not confirm the source for the condition of Chudamani.

"Who did this?"

"Pietra," Chudamani grumbled.

"How did they get your records and those pictures from the hospital?"

Chudamani threw his phone across the room and got out of bed. Danielle stared at him as he slammed his fist on the table. There was fear fueling his anger, and she felt tense.

"How could they!" He shouted.

He flopped in the chair, letting his head fall into his hands. He felt betrayed by a label he had been with for twenty-something years. They grew tired of him just like a child with a new toy. He hit his head with the heel of his hand and grumbled.

"They can't do this," he snapped.

Portia walked over to him and licked his hands. She whined as he seemed to only cause himself pain; it made her nervous.

Danielle called Fiorella to get details about the breaking news. Her phone went straight to voicemail. Her worry appeared more as she watched Chudamani was becoming stressed.

"Fiorella, call me back!" Danielle's voice was panicked.

Chudamani walked to the closet and pulled out fresh clothes. Danielle watched as he stuffed his wallet into his back pocket and grabbed his keys.

"Where are you going?" Danielle asked.

"To pay my respects to my dying career." Chudamani knelt and put Portia's vest on. "If they want to know the truth, I'll give them a show."

"Chudamani, don't do anything rash. You can't afford to do this."

"It's too late. They have footage of us in the elevator, Danielle. Not to mention pictures of me after treatment. The storm is coming to shore, and I can't wait for it to hit." Chudamani opened the door guiding Portia out. "I'll be back."

"Chudamani, please!" Danielle's cry fell on deaf ears.

She growled in frustration and grabbed fresh clothes. She tossed her hair into messy bun and grabbed the hotel key. She hurried down to Vicenzo and Angelica's room and hit hard on the door.

"Vicenzo, open up!" Danielle's voice was panicked.

The door opened with urgency and Vicenzo told Angelica to call for help.

"No, it's not that. Chudamani's going to the label, and he's very upset." Danielle stopped the panic on that emergency.

"What do you mean?"

"The label knows about…"

"I saw it. Come on, let's go." He grabbed his coat. "Angelica, I'll be back."

The two of them rushed down to the lobby and called a car. She stared out the lobby window as they waited.

"He's not thinking straight," Danielle mentioned.

Vicenzo put his hand on her shoulder, and she sighed. Her thoughts were scattered as to what would happen if he went in alone. Vicenzo pulled his phone out and called Antonio to meet them at the label.

"We'll take care of this," Vicenzo said.

Danielle looked at Vicenzo as the fifty-something-year-old had worry on his face, despite trying to be positive. His concern for his friend's career and health were noted by the repeated tapping of his foot.

"Here's the car," Vicenzo said, standing up.

The quick pace of urgency got them into the comforts of the warm car. Vicenzo instructed to take them through the quickest route to avoid Roman traffic. Danielle looked out into the distance while she hoped they would catch Chudamani from making a horrible, career-ending choice.

"Don't worry; we'll get to him." Vicenzo gave her shoulder a pat.

Chudamani stared at his label's headquarters and took a deep breath. He nervously bit at his cuticle with wide eyes beneath his sunglasses. Portia laid her head on his lap and groaned for his attention.

"Go in like the Americans, with both guns blazing," Chudamani mentioned as he rubbed her ears. "Be quick to show them I am capable to hold my own. Defend Danielle's honor and come out with minimum repercussions."

Chudamani took a deep breath, ready to go in, but he stopped at the sound of someone knocking on the opposite window. He turned and saw a child standing there. The curly-haired girl had tattered gloves and stared with pleading eyes.

"Roll down the window," he said to the driver.

The back-right window slowly went down, and Chudamani stared at the icy-blue eyes of the young girl.

"I am sorry to bother you, but could you spare some change, please?" The small child asked.

He reached into his wallet and pulled out some folded money. Portia barked at her and wagged her tail at the child. The little girl reached in and petted Portia on the head.

"Here you are," Chudamani replied with generosity.

"Grazie, God bless you," she thanked him and rushed off.

Portia barked and, without warning, jumped out the car through the rolled down window.

"Portia!" Chudamani quickly jumped out the car.

He rushed through the crowd as Portia chased after the child. He gasped, not loving the cold air with compromised lungs. Chudamani stopped and covered his face breathing deep to catch his breath. His eyes focused on seeing the little girl holding Portia by her leash.

"Carità," someone called.

Chudamani stopped as the little girl rushed over to a very familiar woman. He walked over, and Portia walked over to him. The ice-blue gaze glanced up, and she smiled at him.

"People will talk about us meeting this way," Speranza said. "I see your dog has met my daughter. Carità, this is my friend, Chudamani Amoretto. He is *that* guy."

The curly-haired girl looked up at Speranza and smiled. She moved her gaze over to him and smiled, walking up to him.

"I see I'm popular even in a different type of crowd." Chudamani knelt and put out his hand to her. "Pleasure to meet you, Carità."

"Pleasure to meet you," Carità replied.

"Are you angry over something?" Speranza asked as she walked over. "You have conflicting thoughts. You seem happy, but there is anger about something that just happened."

Chudamani petted Portia, and he took deep breaths as the cold was hurting his compromised lungs. Speranza looked at him and placed her hand on his shoulder.

"You shouldn't be out in the cold in your condition."

"I'm fine; it just takes longer for me to embrace the sudden change in temperature." He smiled weakly.

"You have a good heart," Carità mentioned. "Mama, he gave me five Euros!"

"You may give that back," Speranza remarked.

"No, let her keep it; buy something nice." Chudamani smiled and looked at the young girl's tattered gloves.

He removed his gloves from his hands and handed them to her.

"For me?" She was surprised.

"You need better gloves than those to survive the winter this year."

"That is too much." Speranza knelt, pulling the coat tight around her.

"It's a gift to fill a need." Chudamani reached over and rustled the girl's hair.

"I love them!" She put the large gloves on her hand. "I'll take good care of them, I promise!"

Chudamani smiled as he glanced over at Speranza, and the mother and lady of the night smiled back. He stood and glanced over at the building that still held power over his future. He stuffed his hands into his pocket and sighed.

"Maybe what you are feeling is your heart saying this is not the place for you." Speranza placed her hand on his shoulder. "You have to ask yourself what you really want. Is the stress hurting you more?"

"I'm tired of fighting a battle that can't be won. I lost a lot in the last three years and have gotten nothing in return from them. They see me as a product that has an expiration date, but I have so much more to give." Chudamani glanced over at her.

"Then do what you love. Believe in yourself and the people you surround yourself with. They will give you the hope and faith you need."

Chudamani chuckled a little, placing his hands on his head.

"There was a moment when I didn't think I'd be standing here. The pain alone was unbearable, but the people I love brought me back. I had a moment where I walked towards the light, but I heard their voices. I was pulled back, and things started moving quickly. My body was healed, despite the huge scar I have on my chest to remind me. My hair is slowly coming back, along with my strength to overcome the effects of the treatment. My scans were clear, and I've stepped out into the real world!"

Chudamani took a deep breath through the wool scarf he wore. He glanced over at the young woman and child.

"I gave up a life to live another one. I'm here now, and I'm living with the time I have been given. Though it may not be a lot, I've found a woman who doesn't stare at me like a broken toy. She gives me faith that there are people who can still see me as a man."

"Then there is your answer," Speranza said. "Go with that."

Chudamani smiled and whistle for Portia. She came to his aide, and he grabbed her leash.

"Why do I feel like every time I need to talk to someone, you are there?" Chudamani asked.

"Right time, right place." Speranza smiled. "Go, you have a life to live."

Chudamani walked into the crowded Roman street and walked towards the grand doors of his label. The looming feeling still floated on the air as he made his approach.

"Chudamani," Danielle's voice called.

He glanced over to see Danielle jumping out of the car. Vicenzo got out and pulled his coat tightly around his broad shoulders. They walked towards him, and Chudamani turned to them. He petted Portia, as she slightly groaned.

Danielle smiled but stopped as she saw him stagger. She hurried towards him while he collapsed on the curb.

"Chudamani!" She shouted.

The sudden episode brought the attention of several people. She pushed through the crowd of concerned spectators.

"Vicenzo!" She cried out.

He pushed through and stopped as Danielle came to her knees. She lifted Chudamani's head up, and Portia slid under. She watched as the violent spasms continued. She talked to him as she rubbed his back, but they weren't subsiding as quickly.

"Chudamani, I'm right here. Please, come back." Danielle's eyes began push the tears through.

Vicenzo called for help and counted the seconds the seizure was lasting. Danielle looked at him as the concern of his friend was at stake.

As they finally came to a halt, he remained down on the ground. Portia remained to comfort her master, and Danielle wiped away the tears that escaped his eyes.

"I'm here. I'm not going anywhere." Danielle kissed his head. "You and I have a lot to talk about. You must stay with me. I can't do this again."

Help arrived, and Danielle looked over at Vicenzo, who watched in horror. Portia followed the help, but they shut the doors. Danielle got up slowly with Vicenzo's help.

"Let's go!" She cried. "I need to be there!"

"Come." Vicenzo whistled to Portia.

Danielle looked over and saw Pietra standing in the doorway of the label. She narrowed her eyes at the woman, as Vicenzo brought her to the car again.

"Good job, Portia." Danielle petted the lab as she leaned her head on her lap.

The ride brought concern for the future. She looked at Vicenzo as he tapped his foot eagerly, wanting to be at the hospital that very second.

"God, please let him be alright," Danielle whispered.

She reached into her purse and called Francis to let him know. She looked to Vicenzo to call the others that needed to be there.

"What about his mother?" Danielle asked.

"He doesn't speak with her. She's been absent in his life since he decided to go a different way. And you know his step-father is Antonio. That's the only family he keeps next to Francis." Vicenzo sadly moved his eyes down, away from her gaze

Danielle looked at Vicenzo and reached over, placing her hand on his shoulder.

"He'll be alright," Danielle said.

"He's had these before, and they never bring good news." Vicenzo looked at her with a less than hopeful look. "Did he take his medicine?"

Danielle shook her head and looked at Portia, as the lab remained vigilant to where they were going. She lightly petted the six-year-old's ears and hoped.

CHAPTER ELEVEN

The hours ticked away as they waited to hear something about Chudamani's situation. Danielle glanced around at the hospital, hoping for a miracle.

"Danielle," Francis' voice came through the doors.

She looked at Chudamani's younger brother as he came running in. She stood up, and tears began to fall down her face.

"What happened?" He asked.

"He had an episode, but it was a violent one." Danielle's whimpers couldn't be ignored.

"Ok, it's okay. He'll be alright." Francis wrapped his arms around the woman who cared for his older brother. "He's a fighter, and he has a family right here to keep the hope alive."

Francis looked over at Vicenzo, as he kept his mind far from where he was.

"Let me find out what is going on." Francis sat her down. "I'll be right back."

He walked to the desk, and Danielle watched Francis talk to the nurse at the desk. She pulled a chart and handed it to him. He looked at her, giving her hand a pat, before walking back over.

"He's in recovery now." Francis sat down.

"What does that mean, padre?" Vicenzo asked.

"Padre Francis?" The doctor's voice came.

Francis looked up and walked over to the older man, who was dressed in dark green scrubs. He placed his hand on his shoulder and gave a nod. Danielle watched as the doctor spoke to Francis. She looked at them eagerly, trying to figure out if it were good or bad news.

"God, please." She clasped her hands tightly.

###

The silence was pounding as he opened his eyes in the dully-lit room. He moaned and saw someone sitting in the chair beside his bed. The broad-shouldered man was reading something about the miracles in everyday life.

"Who are you?" Chudamani moaned.

"No one special, really. We do have a mutual friend in common, though," the broad-shouldered man set the book to the side. "My wife, Danielle."

"Oh, God, I'm dead!" Chudamani moaned.

"No, no, not dead. Badly injured in your head. You had two grand-mal seizures that appeared as one. But don't worry, my friend, you'll survive them." Harrison smiled.

He walked over to Chudamani and placed his hand on his head.

"You and Danielle have become quite close," Harrison said. "Very close after last night. I am very proud that she got rid of that doubt in her head. She's become my sunshine again, and I have you to thank for that."

Chudamani moaned as he felt pressure in his head. "You got to stop talking."

"Hey, without me, you two would have missed each other totally. Your stupidity would have gotten you canned a long time ago. Your brother is the one who asked for help with you. You are very stubborn man, Chudamani. I'm impressed that my wife told you to go fuck yourself the very first day, but she did it out of anger. You see, she felt she was being mocked by whatever higher power by putting you in her path. But, because of your friends, she's found that maybe the big man upstairs works in mysterious ways. You got her away from her brother, whom would easily have convinced her to move home."

"Now, I know I'm dreaming." Chudamani lightly touched his forehead. "Please go away. I'm feeling like a migraine is going on."

"That's just reality waking you up. So, before you wake up, I'll remind you to take care of her and let her know I'm right here."

Chudamani looked at Danielle's deceased husband, but a bright light blinded him.

He gasped, and the monitor's around him began picking up his vitals.

"Doctor!" Danielle shouted.

A doctor rushed in with his team. Francis grabbed Danielle out of the way and shuffled her out the room. She covered her mouth as she watched, wondering what was happening.

"It will be alright," Francis said. "Watch."

It was minutes later that the doctor walked out with a smile of success. Francis gave a nod, and Danielle looked at him in question.

"He's alright. He's breathing on his own now," the doctor said. "Go on."

Danielle rushed in and stared at Chudamani, who opened his eyes to stare back at her. Her weak smile brought tears to her blue-eyed gaze. She came to his side and took his hand in hers.

"You are alright," she whispered.

She lightly brushed his cheek and looked over at Francis, who raised his hands up in grateful prayer.

"Hey, dork," Chudamani's whispered.

"Don't do that again," Francis replied as he patted Chudamani's cheek. "You had this young woman scared for your life."

His gaze looked at her, as she held his hand tighter. He smiled weakly, trying to stay relaxed.

"I have a huge headache," Chudamani said.

"It, too, shall pass," Francis joked. "God was with you, brother. I believe he gave you this chance to find hope and faith in this world."

"You have to say that because you're a priest," Chudamani joked.

"No, I say that because it's true. I prayed for you many times to find your way back. To find someone who could understand you, and I believe there were some answered prayers. Danielle was in the right place at the right time."

Danielle looked back down at Chudamani. He gave her hand a light squeeze, content as she stayed close to his side.

"Where is everyone else?" Chudamani asked.

"Vicenzo said something about the storm," Danielle said. "He told me he was going to drop a miracle on you—whatever that means."

"He's a moron." Chudamani laughed.

"Danielle, could you do me a favor and get some water for Chudamani?"

"Sure." Danielle smiled.

She leaned forward and kissed his cheek. She then walked out, and Francis looked at him with concern.

"What is it?"

"I think you should marry that girl," Francis stated. "I know you two just got together, no judgement. I'm speaking to you as your brother, Chudamani. She's been here every day, hoping to see you wake up. It's been a month, Chudamani, and, like clockwork, she's been here reading to you, playing music…your music. Vicenzo and Natalia had to kidnap her at times."

Chudamani looked at his brother and smiled.

"I can't give her what she wants."

"She doesn't want much, just you." Francis sat down. "You make her happy, and I think she'll make you happy."

Chudamani nodded, and he looked away as he felt tears forming in his eyes. He wanted to give Danielle everything she wanted, but it was impossible to do that. Life-changing events limited him from doing just that. He remembered the conversation with Tazia, as she reminded him of his in ability to give *her* what most women wanted.

"What is your concern, Chudamani?" He heard Francis ask.

Chudamani reached up and lightly let his hand touch the bandage wrapped around his head. There would be a new scar that would serve as a reminder of the hardships. His hazel gaze eyed the IV in his hand and the heart monitor attached to his finger.

"I'm afraid she will leave," Chudamani remarked. "It seems to be a trend in my life."

"Danielle isn't going anywhere, brother. You can't get rid of her, and I think you are trying to protect yourself from risking everything for a woman who gave you her sorrow to be leveled with you. Have faith, brother, and let your heart do what's right."

Chudamani saw Danielle peering in and smiled. He looked at Francis, as his little brother sat beside him.

"You'll be here for another week, but I think you'll be happy to know that I'm giving mass in the chapel down the ways to make it easy for you to get there." Francis gave Chudamani's leg a pat.

"You keep pushing." Chudamani gave him a kick.

"I'm your little brother; what else am I supposed to do?"

Danielle walked in, and Francis stood up. He leaned forward and kissed Chudamani's head and, with his thumb, made the sign of the cross, asking for God to watch over him.

Francis walked over and placed his hand on her shoulder.

"God bless you, Danielle." He smiled and walked off.

She looked at Chudamani and walked over to him. She kissed his forehead, and he grabbed her hand.

"What happens now?" Danielle whispered.

"What do you want to happen?" Chudamani asked.

"I refuse to leave your side."

She sat beside him and leaned forward, kissing him on the lips. He lightly stroked her cheek as she laid her head on his chest.

"I'll be right here, Sunshine." He ran his hands through her hair.

Another week went by, and Chudamani was released from the hospital. He was ordered to limit his activity until he fully got his strength back.

"Alright, watch your step," Danielle said as she guided him.

"When are you taking this blindfold off?" He asked, reaching out to feel what was around him.

"When I'm ready to." Danielle walked to the door and unlocked it.

She turned on the lights and pulled the blindfold off, only to be welcomed by friends and family.

"Welcome home!" They greeted him.

They welcomed him with hugs and smiles. He laughed and hugged them, as they gave him flowers and gifts. Danielle walked around them and fed Portia a treat while she begged for people food.

"How are you feeling?" Natalia asked as she wrapped her arm around his.

"I feel good. Still feel a little loopy from the medicine, but it will pass." Chudamani beamed. "I had a great support while I was there."

Natalia smiled and kissed his cheek. She admired the new look, and he lightly patted his head. The scar from the surgery once more gave him a smooth shave. He chuckled, as he was getting used to no longer sporting hair.

"I think she thinks it's sexy," Natalia whispered. "And you look good for being in a hospital bed for a month."

"I'll get my muscle back."

Vicenzo gave him the longest hug and patted his cheek.

"You're too skinny," he teased, "but I know one girl's cooking that can give you back some meat."

He looked over at Danielle, who was talking to Angelica.

"Yeah, she owes me a good meal." Chudamani leaned against his best friend.

Danielle looked over and smiled at him. He gave Vicenzo's shoulder a hard pat, as he went to walk around and visit with the large family that he had.

There was very little talk of work, but music still came to settle in Chudamani's home. He pulled out his guitar and began to play. His band found other forms to play, while Vicenzo and Natalia used their vocals. Danielle walked around as she cleaned up a little.

"Here, let me help," Francis said as he took plates.

They walked over to the kitchen and ran water over them.

"Thank you, Danielle," Francis said.

"For what?" Danielle grabbed the soap and poured it on the sponge.

"For everything. For staying with him through the hardest part of recovery. I know it was hard to see him suffering, but you were a champ." Francis smiled.

Danielle looked over her shoulder at Chudamani, as he just fell back into what he does best. She knew that the news of being dropped from his label wouldn't be easy, but that was not her place. She also knew she was out of a job, because, when they dropped him from the label, she was asked to clean out her office. Their reason was 'fraternizing with clients.' She had lost her job, and, if she didn't find a replacement, she'd be asked to leave Italy as well. Her work visa had been renewed, but that was when she was still with the label.

"What will you do now?" Francis asked.

"I don't know. Since they dropped my contract, I'm to return to the States in thirty days. If another job comes available before that time comes, then I can stay. There really isn't anything for me in the States. My brother refuses to return my calls, and my in-laws believe I'm a traitor to their family name. So, I'm reapplying to change my married name back to my maiden name." Danielle sighed.

"What is your maiden name?" Francis asked.

"Guillot," Danielle said.

Francis smiled and placed his hand on her shoulder. "It will all work out for you. I believe there are things that are meant to be and being right here is where you are meant to be. My brother will find a way, and so will his good friends. They love you like one of their own and will do what they have to to find a way for you to stay here."

Danielle glanced at Francis, as his faith was refreshing to her. She knew Chudamani had not been as faithful since Tazia left him at the altar, but there was something in his eyes. He told her about a strange dream he had while he was at the hospital, one that dealt with talking to her dead husband.

"We'll find away," Danielle whispered.

Danielle washed the plates as she hummed the songs they were singing. She felt at home with the group of musicians that befriended her. She would miss her daily gossip with Fiorella, but there was no way she could have all her friends.

There was a knock on the door, and Danielle walked to answer it. She opened it to see her first friend in Italy, and her gaze softened to see the well-dressed woman.

"Fiorella," she said.

"Can I come and welcome home Chudamani?" Fiorella asked.

Danielle hugged her friend tight. "You are welcome to visit anytime."

"I feel bad about them letting you go." Fiorella hugged her tight. "I want you to know that I went to the mat for you, but that bitch, Pietra, cried to her daddy."

"It's fine; I'll find another job soon. Please, don't bring work up. Chudamani doesn't know, and he doesn't need to know yet."

"Of course." Fiorella held the bottle of wine. "Peace treaty?"

"He can't have it, but everyone else can."

Danielle and Fiorella walked to the living area where they all still played on. Chudamani looked over at Fiorella and gave a nod. Vicenzo was not so forgiving, as he grimaced at the young woman, muttering what both could make out as 'traitor'. That was then replied to by Natalia, who slapped the back of his head for his attitude.

As the evening progressed, the music played on the record player. Chudamani grabbed Danielle's hand and pulled her into his arms, as they danced to the old Italian records. She looked up at him and lightly ran her hand over his bald head.

"I like it," Danielle stated. "I think it makes you more appealing."

"I like my hair," he joked.

"You still have hair on your face. We can cut that off and make a hair piece?" Danielle laughed.

"Not funny," Chudamani said, dipping her.

She laughed as he pulled her up and kissed her.

"I would like to make a toast," Vicenzo announced as he tapped a glass.

The music stopped, and everyone looked at him as he raised an empty glass. He looked at his wife and then looked at the others around the room.

"I would like to raise a glass to my friend for his strong will to survive the last six months of hell…sorry,

Francis. But I want to welcome him home, as we are all glad that he said, 'screw you' to the white light, again."

"You know, I really did it for you, buddy, because you couldn't handle the burning of contracts." Chudamani smiled.

"I know. Sorry, Danielle, but I am and will always be that asshole's first love. We just decided we needed to be friends."

"You're an ass, Vicenzo," Danielle laughed.

"Chudamani, she's so one of us, so you better marry that girl. So, to Chudamani, may he show the world that he is still going strong!"

They all toasted Chudamani, as they continued to welcome him home.

The celebration finally ended, and Chudamani found comfort on the sofa with Portia. He felt drained after celebrating and fell asleep before the ten o'clock hour. Danielle glanced over at him as she cleaned up around the apartment. She felt a slight sadness come over her as she wondered what the future held for the talented singer and herself. They had a new chapter in their lives to start, but the unknown remained a factor for them both.

She sat down and had another glass of wine. Her gaze fell to the picture of Harrison still on her locked screen. She smiled a little, but then glanced up to look at Chudamani.

"What's the issue?" His voice broke her thoughts.

Danielle glanced over and looked at the smooth-faced man. She shook her head, amused by the shaven face.

"I recall that you only could picture me with my beard, but the picture you have on your lock screen is my first assignment with the Marine Corps. I believe that was 2007; I got recruited for war, and you got recruited for the corporate world. We were worried we weren't going to be able to make it to your parents' anniversary party. We also were struggling to make ends meet." Harrison rubbed his chin.

Danielle smiled and laughed. "I think we made it—though late, but we did it."

"Great times. I also recall that your mother told you that 'you better tie down that boy or he'll find some other southern girl.' I told you that would never happen. We may be worlds apart, but we'd find each other again. You southern girls were always worried about tying a husband down, but you got stuck between two worlds…old and new."

Danielle nodded and looked at him as he reached for her hand.

"Haven't you noticed I'm with you yet?" Harrison asked.

"I see it."

"So, what's the problem? You got me here, Dani. Are you worried about him? You should be—he's a crazy bastard—but he suits you."

Harrison reached over and stroked her cheek. She stared in his green eyes, leaned forward, and kissed him.

"So, Sunshine, I believe you have a huge decision coming up. That man is going to need help keeping himself above water. Your friends are trying to solve all of your problems. What say you?"

"I want to stay," Danielle remarked.

"Then stay."

"I have thirty days."

"Look, you have the will, the reason. So, just find the way. Let him help you too. He needs you, and you need him. I'm just the voice in your head when you are asleep."

Danielle felt his hand pull away.

"It's time to wake up, Sunshine."

Danielle opened her eyes, feeling a gentle hand push back her hair. She saw the morning light seep into the front window of the apartment. She then felt a kiss on her cheek.

"Buongiorno," he whispered in her ear.

She sat up from falling asleep at the kitchen table. She glanced up, and he leaned forward to kiss her.

"Buongiorno," she replied.

Danielle stood up and wrapped her arms around his neck, as he wrapped his arm around her waist. Her blue-eyed gaze met his hazel-eyed one, and he leaned in to kiss her properly. She stood up on her toes to meet his lips.

"I have a clear schedule now," Danielle said. "What do you want to do?"

"Spend the day with you." He pulled her close and kissed her again.

Portia barked at them as they showed affection for each other. Danielle looked over at her and whistled. Portia covered her eyes, and Chudamani chuckled and turned Danielle's head back to his.

"She'll calm down in a moment," Chudamani mentioned between kissing her.

Danielle stopped and put her hands on his chest. He wrinkled his brow, and Danielle kissed his nose.

"What's wrong?" Chudamani asked.

"Nothing, but the doctor said to limit your activities."

"Yes, he did, but he didn't see the woman I left with." Chudamani lifted her into his arms. "How can I resist you?"

"Easy, we can find something else to do."

Chudamani shook his head and pecked her lips. "Nope, I can't think of anything."

Danielle stroked his cheek as she kissed him back slowly.

"Shower." Danielle pointed.

"Now, you're talking!"

He carried her down the hall, and Portia followed behind them. Chudamani looked at Portia, and she sat down.

"You have to stay. I'll be okay; I have an extra pair of eyes," Chudamani said.

Portia muffed at him, and he told her to stay once more before he shut the door.

###

Danielle grabbed his hand while they walked down the steps. She smiled at him as he covered his face from the fresh falling snow on the ground. He held tight to her hand, holding Portia's leash in the other.

"Let's take the day for ourselves." Danielle looked up at him.

"I like that idea." He held on tight. "Where would you like to go?"

"Back to the city."

She led him towards the train depot. Her eyes were filled with excitement, and she reached up to kiss his nose.

"You are going to love what Angelica has made for you."

"I'm scared now."

"I'm calling in my side of the deal. You made me change my style, so now you get to have a little different color variation in your wardrobe."

"I bought a red shirt." Chudamani winked at her

"Which you never wore. So, I got you on this."

The train pulled up, and they waited to shuffle onto the train. They walked on, and Chudamani stood while Danielle sat with Portia this time.

He faced her, and she smiled with a devious smile.

"You better not be putting me in a clown suit." He looked over his sunglasses at her.

"Oh, much better than that." Danielle clapped like a child.

"Chudamani," the old lady tugged at his coat.

He turned, and she pointed to the young man. He chuckled a little.

160

"We're in love," the old woman wrapped her arm around the younger man's muscular arm.

"I hope you two are very happy, signora. He looks thrilled." Chudamani looked at the young man with slight annoyance. "I can't wait to sing at the wedding."

"Oh, there's no time for a wedding."

"Elope?"

"Of course!"

Chudamani looked over at Danielle, who covered up her amusement. He glanced over at the commuter's paper to see Tazia sporting her baby-bump on the entertainment section. He slightly gagged. Danielle glanced over at the sight of his ex-fiancée showing off her baby bump.

"Ignore the paper," Danielle said, grabbing his hand. "She doesn't matter."

"You're right; she doesn't have any effect on me." Chudamani lifted Danielle's hand up. "You do, though."

"Aw, that's so sweet! When are you two going to marry?" The old woman asked. "Are you in love like I am?"

Danielle smiled and stood up. She reached up and pressed her lips against his. He slipped his free hand around her waist and deepened the kiss.

"You two don't have to show off," the older woman mentioned.

"I just can't keep my hands off this woman," Chudamani stated, as he kissed her again.

"Silly boy, you need to make her want you." The old woman chuckled.

"Oh, signora, this woman wants me all the time— especially in the bedroom."

The old woman reached over and slapped him on the back of the head.

"Don't be so crude, Chudamani. You save that talk for private, not public."

Danielle laughed as Chudamani humored the old woman. She occasionally looked over at the younger man beside her. Chudamani whispered in Danielle's ear about the love affair between the old woman and the twenty-three-year-old.

"They look happy," Danielle snickered.

"We'll read about it in the paper," Chudamani joked.

The train pulled up to the Roman station, and they hopped off to embrace the city life. He grabbed her hand, as they walked briskly through the station. He led her to Angelica's shop, and Danielle sent Portia to the back.

"Oh, we have been expecting you," Gia said. "Come, Chudamani."

The seamstress grabbed his hand and shuffled him into the back. Danielle sat down and waited to hear what he had to say.

The shop door opened, and a grey cloud slipped in. Her well-tailored skirt-suit and elegant, tailored coat matched the black gloves she wore.

"Gia, I'm here." The shrilled voice of deceit called.

"Well, look what the cat dragged in," Danielle said.

Pietra looked over, and her ruby lips pulled into a smile. She walked over to Danielle and smirked.

"Well, the little mouse *does* know how to dress." Pietra pointed to Danielle's dark washed jeans and white blouse. "You look like you finally got your act together, instead of looking like you walked out of a Picasso painting."

Danielle laughed a fake laugh as she stood up. She stared at the elegant woman, who picked a piece of lent off her coat.

"So nice of you to notice. Natalia helped me pick out some lovely things—especially private attire for the bedroom."

Pietra narrowed her gaze and pressed her lips hard together. Danielle pointed to the wrinkles on her forehead.

"Those wrinkles are not becoming of a woman of your age." Danielle folded her arms.

"Why, you little bitch," Pietra hissed.

"Am I? 'Cause I'm the one who got the man, after all. And we have made love in every possible place. He is quite impressive when it comes to being a man of a certain age." Danielle smiled.

"No matter. He's done in the music industry. He'll never be signed to any recording company again. He's expired in that department." Pietra raised her dark brow and smirked. "And so are you. From what I hear, you have been revoked for an extended stay."

"For now." Danielle stood her ground.

Pietra walked towards the coffee maker and poured a cup of coffee for herself. She looked at Danielle, narrowing her gaze.

"I still go home happy with a job. So, as I see it, American bitch, I've outsmarted you." Pietra sipped her coffee.

Danielle smiled and walked over to her and lifted the hot coffee. She poured a cup and looked down at it, her gaze moving to the stuck-up woman. She had no control and wasn't going to let her treat her like so.

"You are right, Pietra. I don't have a job, but I have happiness and won't shrivel up like a prune with a stick so far up her ass that she needs to find a new lubricant to remove it." Danielle splashed the coffee over Pietra and watched her shriek like a banshee.

"How dare you!" She cried out.

"I'm sorry. Were those clothes expensive? My goodness looks like you need to be more careful when drinking coffee."

Danielle walked in the back, and Angelica looked up at her.

"Brava, signora," Angelica smirked.

"Thank you."

"You have got to be kidding!" Chudamani stated.

"Aw, I think he likes his suit," Danielle joked.

Angelica high-fived her as she walked to the back room. She looked at him in the sharp yellow suit. He glanced at her incredulously and shook his head.

"You promised."

"This is yellow," Chudamani mentioned. "I'll have a seizure just looking at it."

Danielle lifted her phone up and took a picture of him in the suit.

"Well done," Gia smiled. "Now, how about a green one?"

"Oh, I like that!" Danielle laughed.

"No, no, I'm not wearing this." Chudamani stepped down, taking it off.

"Natalia said she likes it. Oh, Vicenzo mentioned it was about time to sport the new look." Danielle read text messages. "Vicenzo also mentioned I made a good choice in color…It suits your eyes."

Chudamani took a deep breath and looked at Gia.

"A deal's a deal."

"Wonderful. It will be perfect for the awards."

"What?" Chudamani question.

"I forgot to mention, I'm your date to the awards."

Angelica walked in and whistled at him.

"I wish I could get Vicenzo in a suit like that. Maybe you'll start a trend." Angelica smiled. "Oh, Danielle, I have a gown for you that I believe you'll love."

Danielle looked at Chudamani and winked at him.

"I'll go try on my dress."

Angelica walked her to the other room where she did most her designs. Danielle admired the designs, and Angelica pulled out a dress.

"And here we are," Angelica said.

Danielle turned and stared at the black gown with rhinestones that looked like stars.

"Is that the dress from…"

"*Amore Mia*, yes." Angelica answer. "I thought it would be the perfect dress."

Danielle looked at the evening gown, and Angelica lifted it off the mannequin.

"Go on and try it on." Angelica walked her to the dressing room she used when customers tried on their tailored outfits.

Danielle stepped into the dressing room and stared at the dress. It was a dress she admired when she first saw Angelica's movie. She unzipped the side and slid it on. It was just a little tight, but she knew Angelica could tailor it to her American size.

She walked out, and Angelica smiled. She clapped with excitement and fixed the train of the gown. Danielle watched the actress fluff the gown just right. She smiled and guided her to the mirror.

"Beautiful," Angelica said. "Chudamani will not be able to focus on anything when you walk into the room."

"Can I see?" They heard Chudamani call.

"No," both women answered.

Angelica smiled and lifted Danielle's medium-length, auburn hair. She twirled it in a bun and nodded.

"Yes, I think this will be perfect."

"Thank you so much." Danielle smiled.

"Vicenzo has a car to pick you both up. You need arrive right at six for pictures."

"Of course, I'll add it to our phones."

"Great!" Angelica smiled and kissed her cheek. "The alterations will be done tomorrow. Chudamani won't know what hit him."

Danielle nodded and walked from the back to see him holding the suit bag. He raised his brow at her as she walked out with nothing.

"No crazy-colored dress to go with my yellow suit?" He questioned.

"Not this time, but there are still other events." Danielle walked up to him and kissed his cheek. "Wear it with pride."

He took a deep breath and whistled for Portia. She rushed over to him, and he hooked her back up to the leash. Danielle zipped up her jacket as she followed behind Chudamani and Portia.

He reached out his hand to her, and she grabbed it. The two of them took the day as their own and enjoyed being out in the fresh air. He guided her to the small music store where he used to get most of his records when he had started his music career.

"Chudamani, welcome! It has been awhile," the store owner walked over.

"Yes, it has been."

"I was sorry to hear about the loss of your record deal. Those bastards never understood how to treat their most highly appreciated musicians." The older man shook his head at him.

Danielle looked at the older man with wide eyes, as he had just spilt the news she wanted to wait to tell him.

"Well, it gives me time to work on new pieces." Chudamani played the news off.

"Very good; go and look around." The owner smiled.

Chudamani guided Danielle through the record collections. He watched as she went through the music he grew up with. He introduced her to several legends that inspired his sound and his style of performance on stage.

"Look at the album art," Chudamani pointed out. "Tribute to the greats."

He slid his arms around her as she flipped through. He kissed her on the neck, and she squirmed playfully. She looked up at him and kissed his chin. He leaned his chin into the bend of her neck and held her close to him as they looked through records together.

As the late afternoon slowly set, the air became cooler and they found warmth at a small restaurant. He reached over and held her hand, as they talked about their lives. There was a new relationship blossoming before their eyes. The sadness melted away from them and left only sunshine and colors.

"I want to help you find a job," Chudamani remarked, "but I don't know where to start."

"We'll find away. I know there will be a need for my services." Danielle kissed his hand.

Portia muffed and sat up. She put her paw up on Chudamani and barked at him. He wrinkled his brow at her. She pawed at his leg, and Danielle felt a concern in the lab's actions.

"Chudamani?" She questioned.

"I don't know what she's doing that for." He remarked. "I'm fine."

Danielle whistled, and Portia came to her and did the exact thing. She looked back at him, and he shrugged. Danielle rubbed the lab's ears and kissed her head. Portia rushed over to him and muffed at him, as she pawed at his leg.

"Portia, sit," Chudamani ordered.

Danielle watched as the chocolate lab stared at her master. She finally calmed down, and Chudamani grabbed Danielle's hand.

"Here we are," the young waitress brought their food out.

Chudamani glanced at the young woman's name tag, and she looked at him.

"Sometimes, we have to have faith and risk everything. Things will work out for you two," she said with a smile.

She placed her hand on Chudamani's shoulder before walking away. He looked over his shoulder, and she was not there. He turned back to Danielle, as he seemed to have missed some time.

"Something wrong?" Danielle asked.

"No, just blanked out for a moment." He shrugged.

He rubbed his head, as if there was a little confusion on what the woman meant. He smiled and kissed her hand.

"I'm alright." He kept his spirits up.

That evening, Danielle moved her clothes into Chudamani's room. He looked at her and shook his head.

"No, those are not going in my closet." He pointed to the bright-colored clothes.

"Come on," Danielle said. "They'll match your suit."

"I have *one* yellow suit now, but you have a wardrobe of colors." He lifted the black and yellow, printed skirt. "I mean, this?"

She snatched it back and opened his closet to the bland colors. She pointed to his black shirts, every shade of grey to black. White to browns hung plainly to one side.

"Where's the red shirt?" She asked.

"That comes out during special occasions." He stated. "Strip teases is one."

She sat down on the bed and folded her arms. He knelt into the comforts and leaned towards her to kiss her nose. She reached up and kissed him on the lips. Chudamani pulled her to him, and they fell into the sheets of the bed.

He stared at her and stroked her soft cheek. His eyes caught the different colors that spread out over the bed. She smiled and kissed him.

"I think I'm in love with you," he said as he pushed away her straightened auburn hair.

Danielle slightly gasped, and he smiled at her reaction. She stroked his cheek and lightly reached up to run her hand over the fresh scar from the surgery. He reached up and grabbed her hand, pulling it to his lips.

"I wouldn't be here without you," he remarked with a softness. "I am saved by you."

She felt tears swell into her eyes and kissed him.

"I love you too," she whispered.

CHAPTER TWELVE

It was no surprise when winter finally blew a fresh coat of snow onto the ancient city and small towns surrounding it.

Chudamani stared out intently, as the cold was a factor to his recovery. He watched as Danielle cooked a feast for company that would soon be filling his home. There was an announcement to be celebrated, along with the nearing of the Christmas holiday.

He slipped his arms around her and pushed her hair from off her shoulder. He leaned forward and kissed her neck, and she looked up at him.

"Aren't you supposed to be cleaning?" she teased him.

"Clean? They're friends; they know how I live." He kissed her neck. "Plus, holding you is so much better."

Danielle turned around and wrapped her arms around his neck. He cocked his head to the side and stared into her blue eyes. A smile pulled at his lips, as she reached up and kissed him.

"Just a quickie," he whispered in her ear.

"They'll be here shortly. Angelica just texted me, and Natalia called me while you were in the shower. So, no. You need to clean while I stir the pot."

He kissed her again and swept her into his arms.

"I've got to keep stirring." She patted his cheek. "Go and, at least, help grab settings."

"As you wish." He kissed her once more before setting her down.

She shook her head and turned around, but he quickly patted her on the bottom.

"Oh, you dirty man!" She squealed at him.

"You have no idea," he joked.

He winked at her and walked to the laundry room, where he used it as extra storage. He reached up above to a cabinet and pulled out the extra plates and serving ware. Chudamani sat them down and stared at the white place settings. He stared at them blankly, standing still.

"Chudamani?" Danielle called.

She stopped stirring and wiped her hands on the nearby towel.

"Did you get them?" Danielle walked towards the laundry room.

She saw him just standing, staring at the plates. She rushed over to him and grabbed his hand.

"Chudamani, look at me," she panicked.

He blinked and looked at her as he saw panic in her eyes. He wrinkled his brow, and she wrapped her arms around him.

"Are you alright?" She questioned.

"Did I…?"

"It's alright; you're ok." She reached up and stroked his cheek. "You should have a seat."

"No, it's not alright!" He stepped back from her touch as he tried to regain his dignity.

Danielle felt her heart pound against her chest as she watched his mood change. She reached for his hand, but he walked around.

"Chudamani, what's going on?" Danielle questioned after him.

She reached for his hand, and he turned around, like he was a different person. Portia barked at him, and he stared at Danielle, the fear in her eyes.

"Danielle," he whispered.

He fell to his knees and covered his face. Portia licked his hands and pawed at him. Danielle knelt to wrap her arms around him. She felt him reach for the hem of her skirt and kiss it. She stroked his back as she listened to him weep.

"It's alright," she whispered. "I'm not going anywhere."

She kissed his head, and he looked up at her. She cupped his face in her hands, staring into his hazel eyes. There was pain and sorrow pouring from them. She wiped away his tears and kissed his cheek.

"Let me help you," she whispered. "Let me take away some of your burden, Chudamani."

"I don't know how."

"We'll find away," she stated with hope in her voice. "I promise."

He took a few breaths and looked at Portia, as she laid beside him, waiting to see if he was ok before she relaxed. He petted her head before standing on his own.

She glanced up at him, and he reached out his hand to her. She stood up and kissed him on his lips.

"I need your sunshine," he said.

"And I'll give it you."

Danielle smiled as she reached up and stroked the past-five-o'clock shadow that surrounded his lips and outlined his jawline. He turned his head and kissed her palm.

"I'm going to finish cooking, and you go change." Danielle gazed at him with adoration.

"Alright," he softly said.

He turned around, and she swatted him on the butt. He turned around, and she winked at him.

"I'll get you back." Chudamani smirked.

Danielle walked towards the kitchen, stared at the burnt rue, and sighed. She lifted the iron pot off the stove and salvaged what she could before making a second batch. Her mind settled on the hopeful thoughts that the new season would bring all they dreamed.

As the four o'clock hour came, so did their guests. Angelica and Vicenzo came first, bearing gifts for the holiday season. Chudamani welcomed them and got them comfortable, while Danielle got changed.

"I heard about this yellow suit Danielle made you get because of a deal," Vicenzo teased.

"I regret every second that I made that deal with her."

"Never make a deal with a woman, Chudamani." Vicenzo gave his shoulder a hard pat. "They always win. Note that I still am not strutting my winter look because the wife hates it." Vicenzo rubbed his smooth face.

Angelica looked at him and kissed his cheek.

"You get what you want, and I get what I want. I don't see it as a big deal, husband." Angelica smiled. "And the suit is wonderful. In fact, I was talking to a journalist friend who'd like to interview you about your situation. And I know the suit for you to wear."

Chudamani looked at Angelica as she smiled.

"That suit is only making one appearance in public, and I'm already dreading that one appearance. So, I'll find another one."

Danielle walked in, wearing the festive, red, fit-flare dress with a low-cut neckline. Chudamani glanced up at her entrance, and his eyes became wide at the sight. Her hair was curled tightly and pinned up to focus on the dress and pearls that draped around her neck.

"Hello, Sunshine," he whispered. "I think this might be an early evening."

Angelica and Vicenzo looked at Danielle, as she stood so confident. Chudamani handed Vicenzo the glass he had in his hand to walk over to her.

"If I didn't know any better, Sunshine, I'd think you were trying to distract me." Chudamani slipped his arm around her waist.

"If you want a distraction, it's not what I'm wearing now, but underneath that you should know about." Danielle kissed his cheek.

"Oh, you are being bad." Chudamani kissed her on the lips.

"Plus, this was one of the dresses I got when I went shopping with Natalia. So, you have her to thank."

"I'll send flowers." Chudamani kissed her hand.

"Well, look who wears red very well," Vicenzo said as he gave a pecked on her cheek. "I'm sure that was to give Chudamani a taste of what is to come."

"You're dirty, Vicenzo. Might need to hose you off." Danielle hugged him.

"You can't wear a dress like that without me making some kind of comment, but you do look nice, Danielle." He chuckled as he hugged her tight.

Angelica walked over and wrapped her arm around Danielle's. The two women walked off to chat, while the men sleeked off to talk shop.

Later, Natalia and her husband came, fashionably late. And Fiorella stopped in to enjoy the company of good friends.

The wine flowed, and the music played. Danielle introduced them to her southern cooking with a flair. They embraced her style of food and were impressed by the time she took to make it for them.

"You have to marry this woman," Vicenzo told Chudamani. "She cooks, takes care of your lazy ass, and got you in a color other than neutrals. Yeah, marry her now. You know a priest, so make sure you never, ever, let her go."

Chudamani looked over at Danielle as she talked to Natalia and Angelica. He smiled and looked back at Vicenzo.

"So, she wasn't a training pony," Chudamani mentioned.

"I retract my statement, my friend. I am ashamed that I saw her colorful nature as just a get-back-on-the-horse opportunity. Although, she satisfies you in that department too."

"You're a moron." Chudamani slightly shoved Vicenzo. "A real moron."

"Yes, but one that encouraged you to take a risk that paid out." Vicenzo smiled.

Vicenzo walked over and handed Danielle and Chudamani a flat, wrapped gift. Danielle looked at him, and he encouraged them to open it.

"It's a little something that fell into my lap last week." Vicenzo sat down.

Danielle opened the gift and stared at an envelope. She opened it and pulled out the thick packet of paper with a record label logo. She wrinkled her brow, as she began to read the job offering as the label's lead translator for any artist of her choosing, plus the eligibility for her visa to be renewed if she stayed.

"Vicenzo," she whispered, nearly in tears.

"I had a friend pull some strings in the label. They are working out details, but you can stay as long as you take that job."

Danielle got up and hugged him tight.

"You need this as much as he does." Vicenzo smiled. "Not just a pervert, I use my sources."

"Don't ruin the moment."

Chudamani stared at the paperwork and shook his head. He stood up and hugged his best friend.

"You have an album to finish, and I need my friend fighting the industry with me." Vicenzo smiled. "They've taken into consideration your condition and refuse to let something like that stand in front of a legend. You start after the New Year, and a signing bonus is attached."

"Grazie, amico. Grazie." Chudamani smiled and patted his cheek.

"Hey, I just know the right people. Meet your translator." Vicenzo pointed to Danielle. "You two make a hell of a team, and my label saw that."

"How come you aren't doing your own label, Vicenzo?" Natalia asked.

"'Cause I've got four kids to support, and they made the deal sweeter when I brought them up." Vicenzo walked over to Angelica.

"Four kids?" Natalia asked.

"Well, it will be four in seven months. See, staying baby-faced makes life a little brighter."

"Congratulations!" Danielle hugged Angelica excitedly.

Chudamani watched as she got excited about Angelica's pregnancy. He stood up and walked to the kitchen to pour a harder drink.

"What's wrong?" Vicenzo asked.

"Nothing, just needed a stiffer drink." Chudamani asked.

"You haven't told Danielle, have you?"

"No, I haven't," Chudamani mentioned. "I'm not ready to walk down that path yet. I don't need a repeat of Tazia."

"Haven't you noticed, amcio, she isn't Tazia?" Vicenzo stared at Chudamani.

Vicenzo frowned slightly and gave his friend's shoulder a squeeze. Chudamani watched the excitement the season was bringing. He already had the conversation with Francis that he couldn't give Danielle what she wanted. He couldn't bring a grey cloud onto the festive holiday.

"I'm going to go get some fresh air. Let Danielle know I'm taking Portia out." Chudamani patted Vicenzo's shoulder.

"Sure."

Chudamani whistled, and Portia came running to him. He placed the harness on her and bundled them both up.

He walked towards the door and slipped out with her. Danielle looked up just as the door shut.

"Where is he going?" Danielle asked Vicenzo as he came back.

"Portia couldn't hold it any longer. It's fine; he'll be back shortly." Vicenzo smiled.

Danielle glanced at the door and felt her brow wrinkle, causing her forehead to crease with worry.

###

Chudamani walked down the slick sidewalk, but he kept his balance as he walked down towards the town. He flipped on a light on Portia's vest to keep the passing cars aware of them. He found a bench and pulled his coat tightly around him.

The town was quiet, leaving Chudamani to his deep thoughts. He found comfort in the coolness, despite what his lungs told him. His ears listened to the silence, but, in the distance, music played lightly on the winter air. The snow on the ground was still pure as a virgin, soon to turn dirty while it melted away. He leaned forward and took a warm breath beneath his wool scarf

"How can I tell her?" Chudamani remarked as he petted Portia. "If I hadn't gotten sick, then this would have never been an issue. Of course, I never would have met her either and probably would have married Tazia."

He clasped his hands together and continued to lean forward. He closed his eyes tightly as he thought of how hard it would be to let her know.

"Isn't it a little cold for you to sit out here and think?" A soft voice broke through his cloudy thoughts.

Chudamani raised his head up and stared at a young woman with dark hair. She smiled at him as she held her hands in the pockets of her wool coat.

"You do know me, don't you?" She asked.

177

"Yes, but I'm trying to remember." His memory was fuzzy from the seizure that hospitalized him.

She smiled, sat down next to him, and pulled five Euros out her coat. He stared at the crumbled money and she removed the gloves she wore.

"I believe these belonged to you," she remarked as she presented the gloves.

Chudamani reached for them and realized he was staring at *his* gloves that he gave a child several months ago. He glanced back up at her and stared at the icy-blue eyes.

"Carità," he whispered.

"Yes, that's me," she answered, her lips pulled into a deep smile.

"But you are grown up." Chudamani looked at the young woman.

"So are you, Chudamani. You gave up a lot, so you could finally stand up against being wronged by someone who tried to break your spirits. I believe that is bravery, and there's honor in doing something you know is hard. You stood your ground and, in return, found something more…You found love." Carità smiled as she reached up and touched the spot where his scar was.

She looked at Portia and petted the lab, smiling.

"Take a deep breath and breathe in the life that has been given to you. It sometimes leads to new adventures and understanding. You had this conversation with your brother. Listen to Francis; he knows what he is talking about." Carità stood up. "Oh, I believe you have met my aunt Fede. She gave you great advice to follow. Trust those who you care about."

Chudamani looked at the young woman as she stood there. He smiled a little, before a deep amusement escaped his mouth as laughter.

"I was blind."

"No, you needed help. You've been given a gift in hope to guide you to enlightenment." Carità stuffed her hands in the wool coat.

"What now?"

"It's up to you. Some people will take their chances and risk everything for faith. So, take a chance, Chudamani Amoretto, and see what gifts were truly given to you. After all, it's Christmas, and there's always time for a Christmas miracle."

"But it's not Christmas."

"Not at this moment, but tis the season." Carità gave a back-handed wave and walked down the icy sidewalk with such grace.

Chudamani looked at Portia and rubbed her ears. He stood up and whistled for her to lead the way back home.

As he made his way towards the apartment, he saw someone standing there. He stopped and looked at the petite figure standing in the cold, waiting. She stared at him as he approached closer. His hand released the leash, and he walked past Portia. She hurried towards him and both embraced each other. They kissed each other and leaned their heads against each other.

"I don't care," she whispered. "I don't care if you can't. I love you too much to let you believe I'd leave you for that reason."

"I know, I was an idiot." He cupped her face in his hands. "I was scared to tell you."

"It doesn't matter to me." She stared at him with her blue-eyed gaze. "You are what I need and only need."

Chudamani kissed her and picked her up into his arms.

"I love you so much."

"Then marry me, Chudamani. Marry me so we don't have to be apart." Danielle kissed him.

"Yes, to that crazy proposal."

Danielle smiled and stroked his cheek. He stared into her eyes and smiled.

"I know a priest," Chudamani joked.

"I know you do." Danielle kissed his nose.

They walked up the steps and walked inside to see them.

"We're getting married!" Chudamani blurted. "Tonight!"

"I guess that's an open invitation to say this is a Christmas miracle!" Vicenzo expressed with hope.

"Vicenzo, get that man to a church," Natalia said. "He can't see his beautiful bride before she makes it down to the aisle." Natalia grabbed Danielle's hand and Angelica's.

"Let's go, lover boy," Vicenzo said, shoving him towards the door.

Chudamani and Danielle stared at each other as they were pulled apart.

"Come on."

###

Chudamani called Francis on the way and explained the sudden decision to not let Danielle go.

They pulled up to the church, and Francis opened the doors, ready to go. Chudamani got out and hugged his brother.

"I think you are forgetting your bride," Francis mentioned.

"She's on her way." Chudamani looked at him. "I don't have rings."

"Here, take mine, I want it back." Vicenzo removed his wedding ring. "It won't fit with those wrinkled hands, but it'll due."

"I have something better. Keep your ring, Vicenzo." Francis walked down the altar and knelt.

He took part of a tassel from the decorations for Christmas.

"It's not much, but it will due." He presented the pieces of tassel to measure Chudamani's finger. "Danielle has a small finger; I can guess."

Chudamani smiled and looked at Vicenzo and patted his cheek. "Thank you."

"You're my brother from another mother. I couldn't let you do this by yourself." Vicenzo patted Chudamani's cheek.

It was moments later that Danielle, Angelica, and Natalia came into the church. She looked back at them as they walked behind her. Natalia and Angelica wrapped their arms around hers, smiling in encouragement.

"Who gives this woman to be married?" Francis looked at them.

"Vicenzo." Angelica gesture for him to come.

He walked over and placed his hand on Danielle's shoulder.

"We do," the three of them said.

Francis nodded, and they each kissed her cheek and stood behind her. Chudamani took her hand, and they all smiled.

Francis performed the late-night ceremony that seemed to take forever for the two of them. Chudamani slipped the tasseled ring around her delicate finger as he vowed to love her no matter what happened.

She slid the tasseled ring and stared at him as she vowed the same.

"By the powers invested in me, I now pronounce you husband and wife," Francis proudly announced. "You may kiss your wife for the first time."

Chudamani leaned forward and pulled Danielle close and kiss his wife.

CHAPTER THIRTEEN

There was no time to fully celebrate their marriage, but that was about to change. Danielle and Chudamani made their way down the red carpet. He walked with confidence in the yellow suit that he promised he'd wear, only to be complimented by hundreds of artists. Danielle was introduced to his musical friends outside of the group she already knew.

"Danielle, a pleasure to meet you," several young artists greeted her. "This one is a handful."

Danielle smiled and placed her hand on Chudamani's shoulder, presenting the two-karat diamond on her left hand that was paired with a wedding band.

"I believe congratulations are in order, Chudamani, you stud." The artist nudged him.

Chudamani looked at Danielle as she smiled brightly. He slipped his arm around her waist and kissed her neck.

"My dear, people will talk." Chudamani smiled as he kissed her.

"Let them." Danielle turned to him and stroked his cheek.

A photographer captured the moment, as they showed true affection for one another. What they didn't expect was that photographer was about to make them Italy's 'it' couple with that picture.

As they made their way to the after-party, they ran into two unexpected rivals—Tazia and her husband, Giacome. Chudamani stood straight as he stared at the very pregnant Tazia and her proud, young husband.

"Chudamani, such an unexpected run-in." Tazia draped her arm around Giacome. "And to see you with your nursemaid."

"Nursemaid?" Chudamani stared at the vindictive woman. "Please, can I introduce you to my wife?"

"Wife?"

"You didn't hear the announcement? Did I forget to send the announcement to your apartment? Yes, my wife, Danielle Amoretto. Darling, I could have sworn we told her."

"Oh, it probably just got lost in the mail." Danielle flaunted the ring on her finger.

Tazia narrowed her eyes at Danielle and smiled as she rubbed her baby bump.

"No matter, he shoots blanks and my husband doesn't." Tazia kissed her husband's cheek.

"Oh, you didn't tell me you were shooting blanks," Danielle said, looking at Chudamani with false shock.

"It was a fluke; you married me." Chudamani shrugged.

Danielle shook her head and reached into her purse. "I guess I shouldn't send out announcements then."

Chudamani paused at the comment, and shock filled his face. She presented him the results of her latest doctor's visit.

"What! That can't be!" Tazia snapped. "You told me—"

"A Christmas miracle!"

Danielle kissed him, and he picked her up in excitement.

"So, I guess I got everything." Chudamani smiled.

"The whole package," Danielle replied.

EPILOGUE

Chudamani stood on the platform at the depot. He stuffed his hands into his tight, dark-washed jean's pockets as he waited. He swayed to the music of the small, regional town. His hazel eyes were covered by the expensive sunglasses, as he watched those joining him on the platform. He was a different man, stronger than previous years. He had found his groove in the musical world again, touring once more with a full schedule. His life was perfect, and nothing was going to take that away from him again.

He was suddenly wacked on the back of the head, and he glanced down at the plastic rattle that rolled back to his foot. He raised his brow and glanced behind him.

"You got that trick from your mother, didn't you?" Chudamani rubbed his head before switching the baby carrier onto his chest. He stared at the hazel-eyed, six-month-old.

The child squealed as he stared at his father.

"No, he did not learn that that from his mother," Danielle's voice came up.

He stared at her as she carried another sleeping child in a carrier.

"I think he learned that from zio Vicenzo, or maybe zia Natalia," Danielle smiled.

She glanced down at the active child in the carrier. She made faces at him, and Chudamani watched before laughing.

"You keep doing that, and we'll have a problem. He'll start picking up those wacky traits, like crazy colors."

"We'll just have to take him to zia Angelica to get new clothes, then." Danielle smiled.

She reached up and kissed Chudamani on the cheek. He leaned forward to kiss her on the lips, before he felt his scruff being pulled.

"And that's why you need to shave." Danielle smiled.

The sleeping baby in the carrier began to whimper. She sighed, and Chudamani kissed her head.

"Switch," Chudamani remarked. "Watch grabby-hands with your hair, darling."

Experienced at switching children around, Danielle took their son and Chudamani took their whining daughter, who found comfort in her father's strong arms.

"La mia dolce bambina," he sang to her.

Danielle and Chudamani stepped back as the train pulled into the depot. They waited for the daily commuters to step off and greet the happy family.

"What beautiful children you two made, finally!" Giorgio stepped close to Chudamani to stare at the beautiful baby girl.

"Grazie. Danielle did most the work when it came to actually having the babies, though," Chudamani responded with pride. "She's a champ at birthing."

"Chudamani," Danielle hissed, followed by a slap.

"For the love of everything that is holy!" Chudamani muttered as he rubbed his head.

"Thank God we're going to see your brother," Danielle said.

"I should put my hands out and get slapped with the ruler like at boarding school." Chudamani put out his hands.

Giorgio chuckled and patted Chudamani's shoulder, muttering, "Hang in there". Chudamani winked at the old man as they said good-bye. He helped Danielle onto the train, minding their son as he squealed loudly.

"He's going to be a singer like his father," Danielle said, reaching for the pacifier.

"I can see his name in lights, 'Raffaello Amoretto, son of a legend'."

"For the brother of a priest, you are not so humble, are you?"

"No, I confess regularly to that sin." Chudamani kissed her head.

The ride to the Roman station was quick, but the getting off the train was a welcomed one. They dashed to the exit, carrying the children through the crowded station.

As they broke free from the Roman station, they took a breath of the freeing air. The fall air was filled with new and exciting things that were brewing for the happy family. The challenges of parenthood waited for them. Chudamani and Danielle had not yet excepted such joys, as they walked down the Roman sidewalks to the fine apartments that hid the old structures.

They walked up the flights of stairs and knocked on the polished door, glancing at each other as they welcomed the next chapter to their home.

The door opened, and Chudamani and Danielle stared at the older man.

"Chudamani, Danielle, welcome." Antonio hugged them. "And you brought the children."

Chudamani and Danielle walked in to see Francis sitting with an older woman.

The older woman had her back turned to them, and Chudamani looked at Danielle, who stood straight.

"Mama," Francis said.

The older woman stood up and turned to look at the company that arrived. Her elegance was complimented by the soft-blue skirt and white blouse. Her hair was nicely pulled back into a bun, and her eyes were as hazel as Chudamani's.

"Buongiorno, Mama," Chudamani greeted her with a kiss on the cheek.

"Buongiorno, Chudamani." She raised her chin up before turning to Danielle.

"Mama, this is my wife, Danielle," he introduced her to Danielle.

"Buongiorno, signora," Danielle greeted.

The older woman walked to Danielle and stared at the squirming child, before she glanced up to Danielle. She reached up and kissed her cheek before patting her cheek.

"You are a strong woman; I know you will keep my troubled child in check. And these babies, what beautiful children you have given birth too. My son has denied his poor mama the joys of helping him. He thinks he's a strong boy who does not need his dear mama."

"Basta, basta, Mama," he sighed, as she laid on the guilt.

"She's right," Antonio said. "Your poor mama has needed her elder son for a long time. Go on, show her your head."

Chudamani looked at his stepfather and removed the sock knit cap. His mother stared at him and raised her brow at him.

"I knew you'd crack your head open, being sick like that." She reached up and traced the scar that served as a reminder of his lowest day. "You have a strong woman, Chudamani."

Chudamani sighed, and she slapped the back of his head. Francis laughed, and Chudamani looked at him and flipped him off.

"Watch your language; your brother is a man of God!" His stepfather slapped him on the back of head. "And you are being a bad example for your children. Stupidio!"

"Still my dorky brother," Chudamani laughed.

Danielle and his mother slapped his head. "Stupidio!"

The babies began to cry, and Chudamani sighed helplessly. He looked at Danielle while she lifted Raffaello and rocked him.

"And their names?" His mother asked.

"Raffaello and Celia."

"How fitting that you would chose those names, Chudamani. It would seem that you have been healed in your faith." Francis got up and walked over; he put his arms out. "May I?"

Chudamani handed Celia to Francis.

"As beautiful as her mother. A beautiful beam of sun that revives us after a rainstorm." Francis looked at Celia. "You are certainly heavenly."

He returned Celia to Chudamani's fatherly hold. He walked over to Raffaello and lifted him up. Danielle watched as Francis smiled at the squirming child.

"Raffaello, you have a strong name and a gift of God's healing. Your father's spiritual crisis fits with your name." Francis looked over at Chudamani.

He returned Raffaello to Danielle and smiled. He placed his hands on their heads and bowed his head.

"Heavenly Father, give these children your love so they may be strong and help those who need guidance. May they be obedient for their parents. Give their parents strength so they may guide them on their right paths. Bless Chudamani and Danielle so they may know that you are with them as they teach their children right from wrong and your word. I ask this in your name, Amen." Francis looked up and smiled.

"I look forward to their baptism next month." Francis patted Chudamani's cheek. "There's a pew with your name on it, Chudamani."

Danielle smirked and kissed Chudamani on the cheek.

"Now that my grandchildren have had a blessing, how about we eat?" Chudamani and Francis' mother patted their cheeks. "You two are too skinny."

Danielle laughed and looked over at her husband. There was a happiness that was restored in his eyes. He had everything he ever needed under one roof. It was, after all, his family and friends who gave him the hope he needed to survive the hard times.

It was the reviving of sunshine that brought new light into their lives.

THE END